Amongst Death

R. Gayle Hawkins

Published by R. Gayle Hawkins, 2019.

AMONGST DEATH

First edition. October 24, 2019.

Copyright © 2019 R. Gayle Hawkins.

ISBN: 978-1393471554

Written by R. Gayle Hawkins.

Prologue

UNDER NIGHT SKY AMONG various trees, David Childers slowly walks down a trail. He cautiously looks around to make sure no one is watching. He learned long ago the biggest mistake he can make is allowing others to see him.

He fastens his jacket as a cool wind crosses over him. He hates this kind of weather. However, he must admit it works to his advantage. Less people desire to be out and about, which allows less people to see him. As well as, the colder the weather, the easier to convince his choice to go inside somewhere, which is where the fun begins.

In the distance, he sees someone walking towards him. Style of dress insinuates a person of male nature, but he knows how that can be deceiving. Oh, he just prays it is the boy he chose. He doubts anyone else walks the trail at this late hour. Yet, there are those odd people.

A gust of wind rushes over him. He shivers uncontrollably. Oh, he really wants this person to be his choice. The cold air is getting too difficult to tolerate even for a man searching for a desire. Thankfully, the distance between him and the person walking is breaking away. The cold may find itself alone if this is his choice. David cannot see the face. However, the body does attract his attention and his choice did state he works on building his body.

As they walk within yards of one another, David realizes it is not his choice. It is a man. His choice isn't a man's age. While he finds him attractive, he refuses to lower his standards. He works too hard at making a choice.

"Wonderful night, isn't it?" inquires the stranger as they shorten the distance in between them even more.

David rolls his eyes. He does not desire to chat with anyone. However, perhaps a quick reply will keep him on his way.

"Yes, but a bit cold."

David picks up pace a slight bit so he can end this conversation quickly. He looks at the ground as they pass one another. Less attention he gives him, the more he shall realize David is not interested in conversation.

"Are you here to meet someone?"

David stops and quickly turns towards the man. This man obviously wants information. Yet, he wonders why rather than wondering who the man is. He fears he faces confrontation from one of those hate groups. He doubts a police officer would ask him if he was meeting someone because he would have the option to say no.

"Let me guess, your name is Steven. I take it you and your organization has worked to dupe the so called "predator". I hate to tell you, but your false identity is safety to no one. Besides, I do not force any of these young boys to do anything they do not desire." states David.

As the man slowly walks towards him, he wonders if he should run for safety. The man does not look ominous. Yet, David feels he should fear him.

"You lie about your actions. The footage is posted for all to see. Do you not feel remorse over their tears? Does the begging for it to stop not touch your soul in any way? Once your triumphant, why do you post the videos? Is it to show your dominance? Or, to keep them your prisoner?"

David's fists tighten as the man moves closer. He wonders how many of the videos this man has seen. Does he know one of the choices and attempts revenge? Obviously, this man does not enjoy the same things as he. So, best to part ways and find safety.

"I do not know what you are talking about! I do not watch the videos you are talking about. You are the only sick person here." shouts David as he turns to leave.

Once David takes a step to depart, the man raises a billy club and smashes it against David's head. He watches David fall to the ground. As he stands over him, he wishes he could simply slit his throat and be done with him. However, it would defeat the purpose. The message needs heard by all. And, with this body, it shall be heard.

Chapter 1

ANGELA SUMMERS LOOKS around her locker to make sure she has all she needs. After a day with dead bodies and no communication other than her own dictation, she does not desire to return because a forgetful item demands so.

She shuts the locker and grabs her bag off the bench. After walking out of the room, she notices Winston hard at work typing the transcripts. Her loyal lunch companion was not there today, but she understands a doctor's appointment is more important than a talkative lunch. Angela walks over and knocks on the desk as she smiles. Winston takes off her headphones after pushing pause.

"I just wanted to tell you I emailed the audio file for the autopsy the police are waiting on. I know there is a high demand for it."

Winston nods and asks, "How did he die?"

"Do not tell anyone!" sternly states Angela. "They were wrong in assuming the head trauma killed him. There was digestion of bleach as well as an injection of some sort. The chemical lab will need to answer what the injection involved. I already sent blood samples off for testing."

Winston cringes with repulsion. For typing autopsy dictation, one would think her stomache was a bit stronger. Angela giggles.

"So, we have a murderer in the area. I will be sure to lock my doors and scout for a dog."

Winston prepares to return her headphones to her ears. She stops suddenly and states, "I almost forgot to tell you..."

Angela feels a pinch on the middle of her back. She quickly turns to see who it is.

"Addie, why are you here? I am going home. Is it not more practical to hunt me down there?"

Addison takes a quick bow and states, "Yes, my queen. However, with the task I shall request, I did not desire to allow a moment of missing you or you ignoring me at your door."

Angela gazes back at Winston. She feels she needs a breather prior to replying. Addison is always so dramatic and she is not sure what he desires her to do. Her luck with him has her attending some event with him and the guy he is interested in. She truly enjoys the events he takes her to, but she always goes home alone after Addison and said attraction depart for his home.

"Addie, why do you not simply ask the gentleman for a date?"

Addie's mouth drops in shock. After gasping, he states, "My queen, I do not know whom you speak of. I simply am required to attend a fundraising event for children with incarcerated parents. As you know, I refuse to go alone."

Winston injects, "I think I heard of the event. Isn't it always held at that large estate outside of town?"

Addison looks at Winston and states, "Considering it is the first event of its kind in our area, it has not always been held. However, it shall be held there, which means many of us will finally obtain an identity to the man who owns it. If ever there was an antisocial man in existence, it is definitely him."

Angela shakes her head in disbelief. She is sure the event is very charitable. However, the man holding it is probably in his nineties, which is the reason Addie doesn't know him.

"Addie, are you telling me I should attend this event because I may meet my future husband that owns a large estate?" jokes Angela.

"If that is so, I want to go as well. Perhaps, he can keep me safe from our murderer." laughs Winston.

"Ladies, you joke about attending. However, from what I hear, the owner is in his thirties and does not have a spouse or recognizable attachment. Unfortunately, I am unable to find out his sexual preferences. He moved away in his teens and is just now returning. According to our town's lifers, he wasn't sociable back then because his parents did not allow it."

Angela and Winston look at one another in curiosity. Angela wonders if she should actually take the event seriously. She cannot remember when her last date was, but it definitely did not spike curiosity such as this.

"When is the event?"

"This Saturday at eight. I shall pick you up. Dress to impress as you know I shall."

Angela nods in agreement and then motions her eyes towards Winston in hope he will invite her as well.

"Oh, Winston, I am sorry to not invite you as well. However, I feel it would create confusion. If people do not find it confusing I brought two women, then they shall truly become confused on which of is Winston and which is Addie."

Angela shakes her head as Winston bursts into laughter.

Winston replies, "Do not worry. I shall be looking for a dog, which means I have my Saturday night planned. Generally harder to grant attention to a man when you have an obedient canine willing listen to you."

"Oh, honey, don't I know it!" replies Addison as he waves and walks away.

Angela shakes her head in disbelief. The night shall be entertaining, but she does not know if she should attend. She hates giving false hope to anyone and some people simply cannot understand she is in now way attracted to them. Perhaps an evening with a dog would be better.

Chapter 2

NICHOLAS PAYNE WALKS down the marble steps and sees heads turn his direction. He takes a deep breathe and prays its the Armani suit gaining their attention.

At the bottom of the steps, he watches the event staff continue working. He exhales as calmness rushes over his body. He knows all of these people will depart his life once the event is over, but he is still uneasy about their arrival. He is creating the biggest viewing of his personal space, which was never allowed in the past. Mom and dad made it perfectly clear long ago that in order for them to survive personal space must have security from everyone else.

He shakes his head to cast away the memory of his parents and begins walking towards the ballroom. The term ballroom seems so odd for him to state. Yes, it is a ballroom by Victorian standards. However, he cannot ever imagine a ball taking place. At least not by him. He doubts the room will ever see much of him after this event is over.

"Mr. Payne, I would like to introduce you to my assistant, Victoria."

Nicholas quickly turns to his right and sees the event planner with some girl. He offers his hand and states, "Hello, I was just looking at the layout."

The short blond hair Victoria replies, "No, trouble at all. They are setting up just as you desired. However, I wanted to talk to you about a possible enhancement."

Nicholas simply nods and waits for her reply.

"I feel you may be able to increase donations through visualization. I would like to print images in large sizes and secure them to the railing on the second floor. When attendees enter into your beautiful home, they will look around. With the images available in the foyer, people will remember they are here for the event and not admiration of your home."

"Very good reminder to keep in the heads. However, what images do you intend to use?" questions Nicholas.

Victoria's smile widens and she states, "I did some searching and found photos of kids that can legally be used. Nothing showing high monetary establishment nor racially barring."

Nicholas looks away to keep her from seeing his anger. The whole concept wars with all he is and was.

He looks back at them and states, "I am sure the images are wonderful. However, we will not use them for I refuse to exploit images of children for gain."

A look of amazement washes across Victoria's face and she states, "The images are in no way exploitation. Simple images of kids at a park or shooting hoops."

Nicholas looks her directly in the eyes and states, "So, in other words, images children of incarcerated parents often do not see. You prove my point against them. The fundraiser is established to assist a child with an incarcerated parent. I understand you feel the images will suffice. However, such children suffer from greater things. I established the organization to assist the kids with school demands, such as student fees, lunches, sports or musical instruments, and necessities, such as bus passes, transportation to visitation, clothes or medical care. These kids have a lot more on their mind than the park or playing ball and it is us who needs to recognize who they are and how we can help them."

Victoria looks to her boss for assistance. Done with the frustration, Nicholas states, "Please excuse me, I am on my way to a meeting."

He does not wait for a reply and begins walking towards the kitchen. He knows he was harsh with her, but she brought it on herself. Pushing open the kitchen door and entering, Nicholas sees two men in conversation.

"Pardon me, are you supposed to be here?"

Both men turn to him. The taller one holds out his hand as he states, "Yes, Mr. Payne. We have not met until now. I am Mikale, the chef catering your event. Next, to me, is my assistant, Jamal. We simply came to look over the kitchen and plan our operation."

Nicholas smiles and shakes their hands.

"I am so sorry for being so harsh on questioning. All these people moving around my home is stressful. I hope the kitchen meets your needs."

"Yes, sir. I do not see any possible issues other than the serving staff, which was hired by your event planner. We will do our job and they simply need to do theirs."

"Understandable, now I shall pray they do." jokes Nicholas with a grimace.

The men laugh together.

"Please excuse me, I am running behind on a meeting with a realtor. And, advance warning, make sure you place everything were it was prior to departure or my chef will take his anger out on me. After I demanded he turn his kitchen over to you and speak at the event, my quality of food diminished slightly. I hate to think of what may happen if his kitchen becomes disorganized and below his standards."

Mikale smiles wide and states, "You need not worry. I am well aware of Peter's demands of kitchen items. When we were locked up together, there was many a night I thought about a shank because of his wrath. Thankfully, the good Lord convinced me it would be wrong."

Nicholas laughs and continues walking to the door. Upon exiting, he looks around and thankfully sees no one. He heads towards the garage. He has not decided upon which car he will drive to the realtor's showing, but he believes it really does not matter. After all his spending on buildings, the realtor does not doubt his wealth.

Chapter 3

ANGELA LOOKS AROUND the ballroom as Addie assists her with her seat. She is glad she chose to wear her Versace gown. She only owns one, but she feels comfortable choosing it for the occasion. Between the ambiance of the large Victorian mansion and the choice of dress of others, she feels in tune with all around her.

The town's elite are in attendance. Addie explained some of the faces within the room, which made her question how he was invited. Yes, the newspaper wishes him to do a story on the event. However, the newspaper also employees writers more familiar with this crowd. Either the newspaper attempts to use Addie's odd perception in the piece or the event holder is hated by someone.

She takes her napkin off her plate and places it across her lap.

"The explanation of event operation I heard is we shall dine with one another and at dessert someone shall speak about the challenges of children with incarcerated parents. I am not sure what shall take place after other than check writing, drinks while waiting for vehicles and, as always, a mob attempting to get close with the event holder. Considering his original stature and what he has become, I am sure the mob shall be large and clinging to his every word."

Angela takes a sip of her water as her meal arrives and replies, "What do you mean by original stature?"

Addie takes a bite from a roll and states, "Well, looking into his background I could find, his parents were not this wealthy when living here. I heard they made money from investments after moving away. Apparently, a lot of money he inherited upon their death.

Rumor has it he expanded the wealth and decided to purchase this place when Old Man Thorton placed it on the selling block."

"Well, I guess I should find a good stock broker and increase my financial structure. This place is amazing and I am jealous." jokes Angela before she takes a bite of food.

"I will introduce you to my broker." states a dark haired man with a wonderful smile in an Armani suit sitting across from her.

She smiles at him as he takes a sip of wine. She does not know who he is, but his blue eyes beckon her attention. She can tell by his attire the comment wasn't likely a joke and by his build, she may desire to know more of him.

"Thank you, but I am not sure I will just yet. May I ask you your name? Perhaps, I may ask for it on another day."

Angela feels her face heating up. Whether it heats up from her spotlight at a table of people she really does not know or attraction, she shall debate later. She simply wants his attention at this moment.

As Angela continues her gaze, the man places his wine down as he chuckles. She does not know why he laughs. However, the sound of it is also appealing.

"Perhaps, place cards were a necessity for the event to run proper. I will take the blame. My name is Nicholas Payne. I am the coordinator of the event and this is my home."

Angela blushes brightly as the entire table laughs. How is it Addie tells her about nearly everyone in the room, but fails to realize the event holder is sitting across from them? She looks to Addison with a smile as he looks as if he prefers to crawl under the table.

Looking back to Mr. Payne, she states, "Wonderful to meet you. I am Angela Summers. Though I doubt the name means anything to you for I am simply accompanying my friend, Addison, and I did not grow up around here."

Feeling her face cool from the embarrassment, Angela begins eating.

A gentleman to her left asks, "Why do we achieve such great honor? At most events such as this, you would sit with a very selective crowd. I know Addison works for the paper. However, I believe the rest of us are simply business owners."

Angela watches Nicholas wipe his mouth with his napkin. She loves his mouth. His lips are not too large nor too small, which compliments other facial features.

"My attempt tonight is to keep everyone's attention on why we are here, which is to raise funds to assist children with incarcerated parents. As Addison mentioned earlier, there is a mob of people wanting to meet me. I am attempting to keep it at a distance and concentrate on why I invited everyone."

As Angela takes a bite, she watches most of the table nod and return to eating their food. She looks over to Addie and begins to worry. She knows the expression on his face means he is thinking about directing conversation, which is rarely good.

"Mr. Payne, I am obviously doing a piece on this event. May I ask a bit about you?" questions Addie.

Nicholas simply nods. Angela does not believe he truly desires to answer questions. He probably agreed simply to make sure his event receives good publication.

"The event itself shall be easy to write about. So, I really only have one or two questions. The first one is about your social status. Are you married, engaged, dating or simply relaxing for a bit?"

Angela wants to hug Addie for asking such a question. She really desires the answer. Looking to Nicholas, she wonders if he shall answer it. Some men do not like defining relationships.

Nicolas replies, "You may knock married and engaged off your list as well as divorced. I am either dating or relaxing, depending on the day and personal perspective. I generally do not place a label of any kind on that part of my life. Labeling it seems to mark it as a task rather than enjoyable moments."

"I understand. I am sure you do prefer to keep that part of your life private. Please do not get offended by my next question. Will you marry me? I feel your lifestyle is exactly what I have been attempting to achieve."

Angela's jaw drops in shock as several at the table choke on their food. She cannot believe Addie asked such a question. She is interested in the answer because it may state his sexual preferences. However, she nor the rest of the table were prepared for it.

Nicholas chuckles and takes a sip of wine. The table of potential donors patiently wait for an answer while looking in various directions as if they are distracted. She knows they are listening. Hell, who would not listen?

"I am sorry, Addison, I do not believe you are what I desire. However, I can help you achieve this lifestyle, if you are willing to donate to my cause."

"I may take you up on the offer." replies Addie.

Angela watches Nicholas nod and start eating again. As the rest of the table continues eating, she looks to Addie.

He simply smiles and nods at her. From knowing him so long, she knows he simply acknowledges Nicholas is not interested in men. How he is certain is beyond her comprehension, but she hopes he is right and she is able to secure some time with Mr. Payne.

Until then, she hopes Addie will calm his questioning so she can calmly enjoy the rest of the evening. And she imagines the rest of the table shares the hope.

Chapter 4

ANGELA SITS ACROSS from Winston as she takes a bite from her sandwich. She knows their daily lunch routine is usually a highlight of her day. However, nothing seems appealing today. Food isn't on her mind. As Angela opens her soda, she feels Winston's intense stare upon her.

"Yes, Winston, the event was very interesting in many ways." states Angela before she takes a drink.

Winston chews the food in her mouth quickly and replies, "Did you meet the guy? Is he your future husband?"

Angela laughs and takes a bite of her salad. She is unsure how much she should state. She does not desire to make what happened an exaggerated story. Yes, she was attracted to Nicholas Payne. Yes, he seemed to take interest in her throughout the evening. However, contact information was not exchanged and she left after a handshake, which is what about everybody received.

"Well, to start the evening off, Addie totally embarrassed himself by talking about Nicholas Payne without realizing he sat across from us. Then, in attempt to ease the situation, Addie asked him if he would marry him. How question such as that will ease any situation is beyond me, but Addie declared to me it was his goal."

Winston's eyes grow so large Angela feels they may pop out of her head. Since she says nothing and continues to chew her food, Angela states, "Our table had wonderful advantage of sitting with Nicholas Payne. We were able to learn more about his fundraiser as well as a bit more about his staff, which is very few people. However, all of his staff are ex-convicts. The gentleman speaking last night was his chef and the ones supplying our meal served time with him."

"Interesting, but does he only hire ex-convicts? Has he served time and feels he is giving back to society now he is rich? There must be some reasoning."

Angela smiles as she seals her soda. After placing it back on the table, she replies, "The chef did comment on Nicholas Payne and his hiring of ex-convicts. Though it really served as a tension breaker for himself. He explained how we were all eating tasteful dinner because of an ex-convict and we were listening to one. He then stated they were all hired by Nicholas Payne, not because he served time, but because he desired good food and someone to talk other than himself. He then went on to explain what the project does, which is provide assistance to children with incarcerated parents so they can somewhat live a life similar to other children."

Winston nods and opens her bag of chips. She places one in her mouth and chews it as Angela awaits her next question. By her expression, Angela knows she is thinking about what she said and comparing it to what Winston wants to know.

"Obviously, a very nice event and I hope it raises some money. However, what did you learn about him? What is Nicholas Payne like?"

Angela takes a deep breath and bites her bottom lip. She can describe his appearance and a bit of his mentality, but she really does not know too much about him. People at the table asked him tons of questions after Addie's incident was over. However, none of the answers were too personal. They all seemed to wrap around business and travel.

"Honestly, Winston, I am still interested in figuring that out. His dark hair contrasts with his blue eyes in a wonderful way. He wore an Armani suit, which displayed his physique very well. And, I must admit, I desired to see him without the jacket and tie. Hell, why lie? I wanted to see him without a shirt."

Winston breaks out into hysterical laughter. Angela notices a few tables looking their direction. She motions to Winston to keep the volume down.

"Is he marrying Addie? Or, did you demand claims?"

Angela shakes her head and states, "No, he stated he was not interested in Addison. And as much as Addie will argue, I never found out if he preferred men or women, which killed the thought of any claim. Not that I really have a chance any way."

"You never know."

Angela chuckles as Winston works on more of her chips. She looks past her and sees Steven Buckham walking towards them. He seems to have her in his eyes, but she cannot imagine why. Their jobs do not work with one another too much.

Reaching the table, Steven stops and states, "Afternoon, ladies. Do you mind if I take a seat?"

Both shake their head no as Steven moves a chair out and sits down. Angela is remotely thankful for his interruption. Now, she does not need to worry about making comments about Nicholas Payne that will bite her in the ass later.

"I promise to make this interruption short. I really only walked over to ask Angela if she would like to have dinner with me on Friday night." states Steven.

Winston quickly shoves several chips in her mouth as Angela looks in shock at Steven. He looks upon her with a debonair smile and awaits an answer. And, she knows he will not like it.

"I am sorry, Steven. I hope you are not offended, but I do not date anyone that works in the same location."

A scowl crosses over his face as Angela continues, "No, we do not work in the same departments. However, I am a very divisive person. Work and its people stay at work. You can ask Winston if you do not believe me. I eat lunch and talk with her multiple times everyday. However, she has never been to my home nor I hers."

An unsure smile crosses his face as Winston nods in agreement while still chewing chips. He replies, "Okay, you ladies have a wonderful lunch."

Angela feels bad as she watches him rise and leave the lunchroom. The whole scenario would have saved him embarrassment if he had asked her without anyone around. She simply wishes this day to end. She cannot imagine it getting anymore interesting.

"Good thing you didn't mention our Saturday morning shopping trips or Addison's often work intrusion. If you had, you may have found a date for Friday evening." states Winston with sarcasm.

"You know those are different. Our shopping trips are the only time we see each other outside of work. As far as Addie, anyone can attempt to stop him from crossing the line, but it simply won't end. He lives a world where he feels he is able to do all he wishes whether there is a right or a wrong."

Angela watches Winston shove another chip in her mouth. She knows her friend desires to say more and she may be correct on thought. However, Angela feels the rules she keeps for herself work splendid and she does not desire to change them.

Chapter 5

STANDING IN HIS ATTORNEY'S large, masculine decorated office, Nicholas reads the last paragraph of a purchase agreement and signs the document. He slides it across his lawyer's desk and takes a seat. He watches the secretary notarize it. As she takes the document and walks away, Fred Durham slides a glass of whiskey to him.

"Wonderful! The celebration drink." exclaims Nicholas.

Fred smiles and replies, "Yes, and my attempt to keep you here a bit longer. There are some items about the new purchase I want to discuss as well as the future one since it shall require more security."

Nicholas takes a drink and places the glass back on the desk. He prefers to keep drinking out of discussions. Exactly what has arisen he is unsure. However, Fred always watches out for his new adventures, which deems this moment a non-drinking moment.

"Well, since I just signed off on the purchase, hit me with the pain you want to bestow. Apparently it is not too horrid for you let me sign the agreement."

Nicholas laughs at his statement and eyes his glass, but decides to refrain from picking it back up even though it is very tempting. Changing his direction of observation he realizes Fred appears as if he suddenly needs to vomit. Perhaps, the whiskey was not the best choice for Fred? Or, is the issue really bad?

"Are you okay, Fred? You suddenly appear a bit squeamish."

He watches Fred take a drink of whiskey and relax a bit more in his chair.

"I am fine. The words you used simply do not compliment what I need to tell you. I am not sure if you heard the news this morning.

Apparently, a murder was committed and is being investigated. The empty lot across from the new property is where they found the victim."

Nicholas cannot fathom importance of this issue. He really should keep up with daily events. However, he finds them too distracting. How can he keep attention on news when there is so much in need among society? Of course, its not as if his parents raised him to care about everyone else. No, it was all about them and their will to keep everything private. Perhaps, he should blame them for his lack of concern for the latest news.

"No, I did not listen this morning. I doubt it shall interfere with our plans. We are in a city and murders do happen."

"Yes, but its not the murder that is so alarming. The positioning of the body and the "poetry" attached is what is alarming. The murderer felt a need to display the body so a warning would be heard. By display, I mean a very vulgar image of a body with parts relocated to areas that are not a common entry point. The police will not say exactly what the warning stated. However, it apparently warns against adults luring kids for sick pleasure. Considering you are opening a housing unit to assist emancipated boys, I am attempting to diagnose a problem before it happens."

Nicholas finds the moment suitable to take another drink. The drink shall calm him a bit and allow him to think. He often sifts through possible conversations in his head when working on projects to prepare for possible scenarios. He did not believe this conversation would arise. Perfect planning definitely finds obstacles even when plotting every aspect.

"Do you fear people may attempt to stop what I am doing? Or, do you fear it will scare away kids needing assistance in living an adult life?" questions Nicholas.

Fred shrugs his shoulders and takes a drink of whiskey.

"I am not sure what it exactly holds for us. The killer may simply wanted to kill and then play with the body."

Nicholas watches him drain his glass and pour another.

"Nicholas, are you not afraid of placing boys in harms way? I thought they would be your first concern and I simply worry about opening with a psychopath in the area." questions Fred.

Nicholas looks him in the eyes and states, "Fred, you of all people, know they are my concern. The way you stated the matter made me believe the murderer was giving out warning prior to our arrival. Opening the facility will take time, which allows the police to capture the killer before we open. However, any threats against those targeting those I want to help, sounds good to me."

Nicholas watches as Fred thinks on what he said. Definitely, a very unusual moment for them. They generally always agree on decisions. However, perhaps there is more to it than Fred states.

"Fred, is this conversation in support of delaying the project? Do you desire to stop everything until the murderer is caught? Delaying our design from opening is idiotic and lazy approach of solving a "possible issue" to me. If needed, I am sure we can make it safer. We have already discussed additional security for the girls unit. Why not simply add those extra measures to this property as well?"

Fred nods and replies, "Yes, I think that would be ideal to calm me. I know you desire to help these kids succeed in life. I simply wish it all to go as you planned. And not knowing the murderer yet, I worry the person will see an emancipated child as an adult and twist his brain to logically kill one of the kids. I know by law an emancipated child is an adult, but we both know they generally still have growing up to do."

Nicholas smiles and nods. Apparently, Fred truly worried about this. He is not sure why he worries. The last place purchased he did not worry about the squatters inside and getting rid of them was a nightmare.

"Fred, relax on it and simply work on adding the extra security into the plans. Besides, before we ever open it, my staff and I shall tour the facility to review what we think needs addressed. Between us and ex-convicts, I believe we can handle any safety matter."

Fred chuckles and asks, "How do you know the murderer is not one of your ex-convicts?"

Nicholas looks at him sternly. Fred rolls his eyes and replies, "Yes, I know you have complete trust in them. I just worry in giving them your trust they may want to display loyalty."

"They did not murder anyone. So, lets drop this and discuss the prospective sights for the girls facility."

Nicholas watches Fred shrug and pull out a folder. He hates it when people point to his staff with negative thoughts. If they were going to point at anyone, he could name a few fitting the bill much better.

Chapter 6

ANGELA VIEWS GARMENT after garment. Unfortunately, none attract her attention to try on, let alone purchase. After a deep exhale, she looks up and scans the store for Winston.

Finding her looking at jeans, Angela realizes Winston seems just as bored. She walks over to her and stands quietly. If anyone is to break this shopping expedition, she deems it to be Winston. Angela is tired of always being the one calling it quits. It makes her feel as if she cannot commit to a friendly activity for long amounts of time or she is unable to find anything to satisfy her. Neither issues are truly a malfunction of her, but it feels like it sometimes.

"Do you feel as disenchanted with shopping as I do?" questions Winston while looking around the store.

"Yes, I am simply not in the mood for clothes today. Perhaps we should shop for other things."

Winston looks to her with a large smile. Angela begins to worry about her suggestion.

"I believe we should go to a restaurant, maybe have a drink or two while we eat and chat. Perhaps, Robbie's? I hear the food is decent and the drinks fabulous. And, since it is more of a bar layout, we may decide upon speaking with a guy or two." suggests Winston.

"Hmm...may be interesting. However, won't your dog get jealous if you bring someone home?"

Winston purses her lips and stomps one of her feet. Angela cannot help laughing. She appears as a schoolgirl who just lost a popularity contest.

"Angela, I honor your odd regulations of keeping personal life separate. Yet, I feel we should connect more. You never go out and have fun. And, do not attempt to argue the matter. If you do, I shall call Addison and have him argue with you as well."

Angela rolls her eyes and states, "Fine, I will go. However, do not think I shall welcome every man attempting to sit with us."

Winston smiles and nods. They begin walking out of the store when a younger man walks up to them. He is all smiles while he looks them up and down.

"Hello, ladies. I could hear you speaking just a second ago and wanted to introduce myself. I am Javier Alexander and would love to join you at Robbie's. I am willing to make the whole event my treat."

Angela looks him in the eyes in desperate attempt to see the type of man he is. Why would a guy they do not know decide to escort and pay for them to entertain themselves? What does he want from the whole event?

"I am sorry, Mr. Alexander. We do not randomly dine with people we do not know."

Still smiling, he replies, "Define a person you know! Many people hide from their true selves. I am simply attempting to know two beautiful women a bit better. I am sure you wish your boyfriends were asking to take you rather than I."

Winston blurts out, "Well, we really..."

Before she can continue, Angela turns to her with eyes of vengeance. She prays Winston truly understands.

"As I said, Mr. Alexander, we do not randomly dine with strangers."

Angela watches him pause in thought. She hopes he will simply give up. Situations such as this always stress her. She knows her youth created the torment. However, men in society simply continue her torture. She just wants away from it.

"Perhaps, we can meet another day. A lunch through the work week? You can think of it as a business meeting."

Angela internally cringes at the thought. The man is attractive and attempts to be polite, but she just doesn't care to know him. She is not sure why she does not want to know him and does not care to find out. She takes a deep breathe and thinks of a reply since Winston has gone completely silent. Though she cannot blame her after the view she had a minute ago. She is sure Winston desires to know why talking with men at the restaurant is fine, but this man joinging them and paying the bill is not okay.

As she is about to answer, she hears, "Angela, I am so happy I found you. I was able to cancel the meeting."

She feels an arm around her shoulder and smells great cologne. However, she is afraid to look. She knows it is not Addie because he would simply tell Mr. Alexander to go away in a rather intimidating way. Oddly, she thinks the voice she hears is the rich, handsome Nicholas she dreams about. The thought of it being him is absurd. If it is, then this is definitely a dream and she needs to wake up before it becomes pornographic.

Angela smiles as she turns to look at the mystery man. On seeing him, she is not sure what to state. He is actually here. The dark hair and bright blue eyes retain her smile, but she desires to laugh at the absurdity of the moment. He makes it appear as if they know each other very well and he is willing to throw off obligations just to be with her. She desires to kiss him for the performance.

"Wonderful news, Nicholas. Winston and I were discussing lunch. Mr. Alexander introduced himself and invited to treat us at Robbie's."

"I am sorry, Mr. Alexander. I already made reservations and simply for three people. Winston and I have a lot to catch up on. I have not seen her in years. She always seems busy when I am spending time with Angela. And seems to hoard Angela at moments

I do not get to participate in. Its not a complaint, I simply feel I miss a part of Angela's life and Winston is the one who seems to have it."

Angela holds her smile as Nicholas laughs. She looks to Winston and sees her amazed expression. If this is a dream, she would rather not wake up. Even if it does become slightly pornographic.

"No problem, sir. Have a wonderful afternoon!"

Joy rushes over Angela as she watches Mr. Alexander walk away. And, oddly, she hopes Nicholas' arm does not leave her shoulder. For some reason, she does not feel a need to create boundaries with him. She is sure it is because there really is no relationship. Simply odd moments that are enjoyable.

Angela looks to Winston and states, "I am sorry for giving you such an evil glance. I simply did not desire for him to join us."

Winston giggles and replies, "No, issue at all. Now, can you introduce me to my long lost friend that wishes I did not take so much of your time?"

Angela and Nicholas laugh and look at one another. The look of enjoyment in his eyes makes her wish to pull him close and let passion take over. She feels her temperature rise and looks away to cool off.

"Winston, this is Nicholas Payne. He is the gentleman establishing residence for emancipated children. Nicholas, please meet my co-worker and shopping partner, Winston Howell."

Nicholas nods and shakes her hand. Angela knows he desires to comment on her name. Everyone comments on Winston's masculine name.

"And to answer your question on the name before asking it, I shall tell you Winston's father demanded to name his first born after his great-grandfather. She never found out exactly why. It simply is what he demanded and her mother gave up fighting about the matter."

Nicholas chuckles as Winston attempts to hide her embarrassment. Angela knows its not the story or the name. Winston simply wishes she knew the why her father demanded it.

"Well, I have taken a bit too much of your time. Though, if you like, you ladies are more than welcome to join me for lunch at my home. My normal chef is back in action."

As he looks at both of them, Angela responds, "We shall be glad to join you."

"Wonderful, I shall see you there."

As Nicholas takes his arm off her shoulder and walks away, Winston moves in close and asks, "Are you torturing me or offering a sample?"

"I really do not know. I suggest we get to your car and find out."

Without saying anything, Winston grabs her arm and pulls her in the direction of the car. They quickly work to exit the mall and partake in a new adventure.

Chapter 7

"NOW, LADIES, DO NOT feel you need to limit your consumption of this wonderful dessert. By my wonderful planning of your meal, you're able to splurge."

Winston and Angela break into laughter as Nicholas shakes his head. After the plate is set in front of her, Angela views the wonderfully ornate cheesecake. The presentation is truly beautiful. With raspberries balanced on top, whipped cream designed to lure your attention away from eating and the raspberry sauce splashed decoratively on the plate, she is not sure where to take the first bite.

"Thank you, Peter. I am sure we all shall enjoy this wonderful dessert. Do you have more in the back if this plate is not enough to satisfy?" inquires Nicholas with devilish look in his eyes.

Angela watches Peter stiffen his stance and roll his eyes as he turns to Nicholas.

"Ladies, please excuse my aggressive tone. Nicholas, you know you are simply hiding your desire to raid my kitchen and eat the remainder. I will not have it. You need to watch your intake. Therefore, as always, the remainder is locked away and only I hold the key."

Nicholas chuckles as Peter departs the room. Angela wonders what kind of relationship they have. Obviously, not a strict one of employee and employer. Though it seems odd to believe they entwine their personal lives with each other. She cannot imagine the two hanging out and scouting women, but perhaps they do.

"He is always dictating my health through food and exercise. I think I shall hire an obese chef next time." states Nicholas.

Angela giggles at the thought and prays Peter shall always work for him. In more casual attire today, her view of his physique is much better and she is enjoying it even more than last time. Rigged arm muscles and dominating chest muscles make her wish for a very drastic change in temperature to cause him to lose his shirt. And, perhaps, a bit more clothing as well.

Winston takes a sip of her wine and then pats her mouth with her napkin.

"Tell me, Nicholas. What kind of business are you in? You are obviously in a profitable one based on what we have seen of your home."

Haven't even picked up his fork yet, Nicholas replies, "I am not in any business other than my charitable work. To keep it all simple, I shall tell you my parents earned some money and invested it in some technological enterprises in their early stages, which earned a very large amount of money. On their passing, I inherited it all and through additional investments made even more money."

"Impressive! Wish my parents had done so." states Winston.

Angela watches as he slightly grimaces and then takes a bite of his cake. She imagines the thoughts of his dead parents are not moments of joy. However, the expression seemed as if he wanted to say much more about them.

"Sorry to hear about your parents. How did they pass away? Was it at different times?" inquires Angela.

With a smile, Nicholas looks to her and states, "No, they were both killed in a car accident. A major car wreck on I-80 during a snow storm took them. They were returning from a ski trip in Vermont."

Angela nods and takes a bite of her cake. She saw no pain in that statement, which is a bit odd. Well, to her it is a bit odd. She does not adore her parents at times, but talking of an accident that killed them would upset her. He seemed calmer stating the accident than where his money came from. Maybe, he is bitter from something the money caused in his childhood. She imagines they often took more trips skiing than just the one. Perhaps, he was left behind. After all, he would still have school.

Bored of the brief silence, Winston asks, "What exactly are your charitable causes? Angela told me about the one taking place now for emancipated kids. I take it you have others from what you stated."

Angela looks down to her plate as Nicholas replies, "There are various things. I participate in various fund raisers, one of my foundations is to assist ex-convicts with education and employment to better their lives on release, another foundation establishes assistance for domestic violence victims and my first foundation I ever established assists runaways."

Angela freezes as tears form. Her hands begin to shake. She drops her fork and places her hands on her lap.

Having gained his attention, Nicholas questions, "Angela, is something wrong?"

Keeping the tear build-up from falling down her cheek, Angela looks to him and states, "No, I just was reminded of my brother when you mentioned runaways. Just a sad moment in my life. However, I am happy someone as yourself is willing to assist them. I am not sure exactly sure what you assist with, but I can imagine it is beneficial to them."

Angela begins to blush from her idiotic statement. She rambled like a moronic jester.

Winston injects, "Please excuse me, I am going to go to the restroom."

Angela looks to her and nods. She wants to hug Winston for offering a chance to break from this moment. She will allow Nicholas to do it though because thinking of another topic is not in her mind's ability at the moment.

"Your brother was a runaway? Did he ever come home?"

Angela's jaw clenches as she looks to Nicholas. The subject is not fond for her and she really does not desire to talk about it. Upon viewing him, she relaxes a bit. He has an expression of worry and knowledge of pain in his eyes. She was not expecting to see it from him.

"At times, he did return, but then he did not. My parents feel he learned self-reliance throughout the several other times which enabled him to finally not return."

"I pray they are right. Rough world that runaways must live within. The wrong people act as if they want to help them and the ones truly desiring protect them can only do so much before accusations of assisting their actions."

Angela knows she should say more about the whole situation. However, she does not want to interrupt the day with this discussion.

"Thank you, I pray often for him. Perhaps, one day, he will appear and we can be friends again."

As Angela takes a bite of her cheesecake, Nicholas reaches in his pocket and pulls out his wallet. She is not sure what he is doing. She watches as he pulls out a card and hands it to her.

"Please take this card. You will find my personal contact information on it. If you ever need to talk or a distraction, call me. I truly do not mind what time of day it is."

As she takes the card, she sees his concern. Its not alarming nor a false sense of empathy. She is not sure how she should define it, but she appreciates it.

"Thank you."

Chapter 8

THE CLUB IS HOPPING tonight with the DJ spinning crazy tunes and drinks going down like water. Ebony Richards feels the sweat rolling down her temples and knows she simply needs a bit of fresh air. Since one of her social media friends is due to arrive soon, she exits the dance floor after giving a polite wave to the guy she partnered with.

Moving through the non-dancing crowd taking up space and tables situated around the room, she really desires to let off a smoke bomb simply to clear the floor. She has seen it like this in the past, but the DJ tonight is not nearly as good as some of the other shows. People must desire entertainment. That alright, she is willing to serve entertainment up after the club closes. Her and her fine girls will get the money rolling in.

She steps out of the entrance into the empty street. The cool breeze is wonderful. She fans herself a bit as she looks up and down the road. For such a crowd at the club, the streets are empty. She thinks there should be a bit more movement. Yet, all she sees is some guy walking towards her. She wonders if it is her social media friend.

She would call out his name to see if it is him. However, she really does not know it. Best rule to keep on social media is do not tell anyone anything other than what they need to know. She does not need his name and he definitely is not getting hers.

As she continues to look down the street, she takes more notice of the man walking towards her. She believes he is the one she is waiting to arrive. His attire is nice and he is well groomed. Nothing she would brag about to friends if she accompanied him, but presentable.

He stops in front of her and asks, "Are you my wild child awaiting my arrival?"

Ebony smiles wide and moves closer. She knows she needs to taunt the desire in order to get the best payout.

"Yes, if you are my stallion waiting to be ridden."

She despises the names she has to use to keep her identity hidden. However, she knows she cannot show it.

"Can we move to a more secluded location? With only us on the street, we attract attention from those driving down the road. I prefer to have a conversation with you prior to any other interaction."

Ebony wishes to tell him to simply talk. However, he is a bit right about the street and she does not desire to be noticed talking to him. She looks around to see where there is privacy. The club will not offer any kind of privacy and talk overheard could diminish his selection, which will probably anger him.

"How about the tiny alley next to the club? The only thing down there is trash. And if any of the club employees exit the door down there, they will not say anything because they know me."

The man does not smile at the suggestion, but begins walking towards the alley way. As Ebony follows him, she watches his every move. She does not care for surprises.

Stopping shortly after entering the alley way, the man stops and turns to her. She looks down the alley to make sure no one is down there. Looking back to him, she asks, "What exactly do you desire to discuss? I told you how my process works and that you shall have first selection."

"I simply desire to verify the security of your operations prior to partaking. I, like many others, cannot get caught in actions such as this. If anything like that should happen, it will ruin my life and anger me to go after the cause of it."

Ebony wishes she could laugh in his face. He may not dress above most of society, but he sure acts as if he is above it. She hates men like him. Always thinking about self, but fails to look at what their actions cause themselves.

"I can assure you safety. I grew up in this life and simply took over after my father went to prison. My location is very secure as is my girls' mouths."

The man nods his head with an uneasy look. She wonders if this is his first time purchasing pleasure.

"Then, let us begin interaction. I desire to know them a bit before making my selection."

Ebony smiles and replies, "Follow me and I will take you around the club to meet each one."

She turns from him and begins walking towards the street. She feels him following her closely. She prefers him to keep a distance, but how packed the club is tonight, she needs him to remain close.

As she attempts to step out into the street, she suddenly feels a clothe over her mouth as his body surrounds her. She struggles and tries to scream, but cannot break free from his hold. She smells chemicals on the clothe and attempts to not breathe them in.

With every fighting move failing and the necessity of oxygen, Ebony begins to cry and shake. The chemicals begin working on her. She feels the world spinning as he moves back into the alley. As she attempts a scream, she passes out.

Chapter 9

ANGELA ENTERS HER WORKPLACE with a smile across her face. The weekend was peculiar and wild. She enjoyed so many aspects of it. Yes, there were moments she did not totally enjoy, such as the man in the mall or the memory of her brother. However, all the other moments were very enjoyable. She even thought of entering Winston's home to chat about their time with Nicholas after it was all over.

Feeling the thought of him heat her up, she knows he is definitely not appropriate topic for lunch today. Not that she usually plans lunch topics, but apparently he is a topic to avoid for today.

"Good morning, Angela. Mr. Baker shall like to see you prior to you beginning your day." states the receptionist as Angela walks past her desk.

Angela turns around and asks, "Should I worry? I know it is not time for any type of review."

The receptionist smirks and replies, "No, he desires to change your workload today and needs to speak to you about it."

Angela nods and begins walking to his office. She cannot imagine why he needs to tell her about changing her workload when she does not even know her workload. She does autopsies. Her workload is defining why the dead died. She doubts the amount of bodies changed drastically and requires her to work more. Or, even less!

She sees his door is open as she continues to walk. She will just peek inside to make sure he is in there and she is not interrupting anything. With a small step to inch close to the entry, she slowly cranes her neck to see him sitting at his desk writing.

"Angela, do not stare at me like one of my children hoping to sneak a yes out of me for what they desire to do." states Mr. Baker as he continues to write.

Angela relaxes and walks into the room. She was not attempting to sneak anything out of him except what he wants to talk about. Perhaps, she should explain why she peered in like she did because it was slightly inappropriate. However, he has yet to take his eyes off what he is writing, which is totally inappropriate. She walks to the chair in front of his desk and sits down.

He looks up at her and states, "Please give me one moment and I shall tell you why I requested you this morning."

As Angela nods, he jumps out of his chair and quickly closes his door. Angela feels her body tense. Is she being fired? Why all the secrecy?

As he returns to his seat, Mr. Baker states, "I am sorry for how this must all appear to you. I assure you that you have done nothing wrong."

"Good to know, Mr. Baker."

"I imagine you remember a recent autopsy you completed. The body of the murder?"

"Yes, I remember it very well due to oddity in it."

She watches a smile cross his face. She cannot imagine why anyone would seem happy about their conversation. However, if it makes this a quick conversation, then so be it.

"Well, you shall see a bit more oddity. Another murder victim was found. The police do not know if it is the same murderer or if the crimes are connected. However, they desire to keep as much as possible out of common knowledge of the public. I promised them you shall do all the autopsies they feel are possibly related. I am very confident in your ability to keep what you find very secure. This shall not add to your workload. We will simply alter all assignments of possible victims to you."

Angela sits back and thinks upon it all. She does not mind being assigned all of the cases nor keeping her mouth shut about it. She simply wonders if there is a serial killer in the area. If so, who and why?

"Alright, I think I understand what they desire. My mouth shall be closed. Have you talked to the transcriptionists as well?"

"Yes, I forgot to mention it. You shall hand all your audio to Winston since she did the last one. If either of you feel you need to chat with someone about the cases, you may speak with each other or my door is always open. I imagine this may become very troubling if it turns out to be a serial killer."

As Angela looks at him, she wonders why he appears so excited. He must enjoy the mystery of who done it. Or, perhaps he is excited his office is able to support the police in a case other than accident or suicide.

"Now, if you feel you cannot handle the cases, tell me now and I will assign someone else."

"Why would I not be able to handle the cases?" asks Angela.

Mr. Baker taps his fingers as an odd look develops in his eyes. He looks as if he would love to blurt out something, but is remaining silent to be nice. She is feeling as if she is in high school once again.

"When you see the body, you will understand. This one is not in the same condition as the other. This time the victim is a female. They do not know how she died. However, on finding her, she had various photos of missing girls stapled to her chest and abdomen. Stapled to her forehead was the address these girls were located. Apparently, the victim was their pimp and the operation was not a mutual desire. To control some of them, she used violence or drugs. She even had a few young illegal immigrants she was training to enter into prostitution."

"Dear God, I can understand why you want to keep this under wraps. Do the police have any idea why this is happening? Obviously, the murderer has a vendetta concerning sex."

Mr. Baker shrugs his shoulders and shakes his head. Angela is confident he would tell her if he knew anything. Besides, according to him, he is happy to talk about any of her concerns. So, why would he not tell her things she desires to know?

"I know many shall find the whole mess horrible, but I honestly do not know whether to cheer the killer on or not. The first murder was deplorable, but this one I can truly understand." states Mr. Baker.

Angela's eyes narrow as she asks, "Do you not believe it would be better if the victims' crime was handled by a court of law?"

Mr. Baker's smile drops from his face and he begins to stammer, "Oh, yes, most definitely better handled legally. I simply agree that those the killer is targeting is appropriate."

"Well, what if the killer makes a mistake and kills an innocent person? Or, what if the person is mentally ill and cannot truly handle their actions properly? Then, there is always a possibility the killer was raised to believe how they are living is correct. Can you blame someone who is taught evil things are the proper operation of mankind?"

Mr. Baker takes his hands off his desk and sits back in his chair. Angela knows the questions are tough for anyone to answer. And, she really doubts many in society ever think about it. Society's operation was determined long ago and very few ever think of changing it.

"Very appropriate questions to ask, Angela. I am not sure if you can appropriately answer all of them."

Angela looks to the ground disappointed. She gave him the opportunity to state his beliefs. Instead, he runs to the safety answer and avoids thinking about any of it. She misses her conversations with Skip. Her brother always discussed things like this with her. He taught her to define herself through thoughts and actions rather than stroll through life as if nothing is taking place other than self. She wishes many people could see his brilliance. Especially, her father for he never cared to listen.

Angela rises from her chair and states, "I am going to begin my work. If you need to talk to me, you know where to find me."

"Just remember to keep your mouth closed about what you find today."

Angela nods and heads out of his office. Her day started off very well and exciting. Now, she is in a major emotional downer and heading to work on someone who cannot talk. Perhaps, Nicholas is the best topic of conversation at lunch today.

Chapter 10

A DIM LIGHT SHINES within the living room as Mozart streams throughout the apartment. Angela takes a sip of her wine as she relaxes on the couch. She wants to discard all of her work today from her mind and this is the best way. The music clears her mind of thought and the low light level relaxes her. She can think of many other ways to relieve stress. Yet, this is her most common one for it requires no one else.

She hears a knock at her door and closes her eyes. Whether it is a neighbor or the murderer, they are taking their own life in their hands for she may lose it and assault them for disrupting. She sits her glass down and rises to answer the door.

Another knock is heard and she has an idea of who it may be, but she will make no assumptions and answer the door. She arrives at the door and pauses before looking out the peephole. In her mind, she hopes it is another moment where Nicholas magically appears and whisks away all of the negativity of the day.

She looks out the peephole and realizes her assumptions were correct. She unlocks her door and opens it.

"Addison, can you not call me before simply arriving? You know I would be forced to open the door whether I desired to do so or not because it is the only way to stop your knocking."

Addison smiles widely and replies, "Oh, do I interrupt a volatile moment of your day? Drink something stronger than wine and get over it."

Angela glares at him as she opens the door wider and allows him in. She closes the door and watches him walk towards the couch while he appears to search for something.

Angela leans against the closed door and asks, "What are you looking for?"

Rather than hear an answer, Angela realizes his motive when he picks up a remote and lowers the volume of Mozart to a barely audible level.

"If any man is keeping your attention here, it shall be me." states Addison as he drops the remote on the couch.

Angela smiles and replies, "Is that your attempt to make me find your competition? You know if I truly work at making connections with men and you work at fighting those connections, your sex life will become non-existent."

Addison lets out a fake laugh and states, "Oh, my princess, you must learn about my ability of converting men. You may have them for a moment, but I shall retain them."

Angela shakes her head while walking to her couch. She drops down and reaches for her wine as Addison sits in a chair. She takes a drink and sits the glass back down.

"Ok, Addie, why are you here tonight?"

"You're finally going to ask me? I cannot believe you even wonder why I am here. My wonderful grapevine informs me of a magical moment at a mall that had you and Winston running for a vehicle."

Angela begins to blush. She did not think of telling Addison of what took place. They usually tell each other everything about men they find attractive. She simply remained in the moment mentally and forgot to tell him about it.

"I am sorry, Addison. I forgot to call you and tell you about the wonderful afternoon we had at Nicholas Payne's house."

Addison's jaw drops as he grabs the arms of the chair. Angela laughs and states, "By the way, his chef is wonderful. I think you shall recall him. He was the man speaking at the event we attended."

Angela watches Addison grind his teeth as she picks up her wine and sits back. He begins tapping his hands on the arms of the chair. She knows he is calming himself and it is hilarious.

"Angela, I came over because I heard about a man who just did not desire to eat alone and another man assisting you in getting rid of him. With your running to the car after Nicholas Payne's departure, I thought you and Winston avoided that killer. Now, you tell me you had a wonderful afternoon!"

Angela giggles and takes a sip of wine. To keep this conversation at a normal level of sound, she needs to think about what to say. Otherwise, Addie will jump out of his seat while taking the conversation to a shouting level of communication and the neighbors may call the police.

"Addie, I simply forgot to call you about it. I was in such shock of it my mind was in a trance afterwards, which was killed at work today."

Addison relaxes his body and states, "So tell me what took place."

"I do not know how you deem the one guy as someone who did not desire to eat alone, but I would rather look past that moment. After his departure and introduction of Winston, Nicholas invited us to share a meal at his house. Winston's gawking at his home caused him to give us a brief tour of the downstairs, which was followed by a meal. Once it was over, we chatted a bit and eventually Winston had to leave due to her dog. Unfortunately, I was required to leave as well since it was my week to drive."

"I shall write a thank you note to Winston for limiting your time there without me. What did you talk about? By what my friend told me, one would think you have a very romantic relationship and Winston is a long lost friend. I explained the whole thing was an act. However, that simply tossed him into accusations of jealousy and took us completely off the topic. I imagine I am missing part of what happened because of the argument, which is why I appear before you."

Angela finishes her wine and places the empty glass on the table. She draws her feet up under her on the couch and twists her body to look at Addie. She feels as if she is empowered by Nicholas to take hold of Addie's attention and for once control their conversation.

"Most of the conversation was about him and his adventure through life. Thanks to Winston, I now know he does not work within a company of any kind nor run one. His parents left him a large amount of money on their death and he works on various foundations he established."

Addie develops a scowl and states, "Wonderful to know. Tell me, how did his parents earn the money?"

Angela is taken aback at the question. Addie looks as if he is searching for something of great importance. She wonders if it is simple curiosity or something else.

"Addie, I hope you are not interviewing me to acquire information on Nicholas for your article."

"Girl, I know you do not subscribe. However, you should at least realize the article is already written and published. A whole week has passed since the event we attended. I am slow at some things, but not writing."

Angela's posture shrinks a bit from embarrassment. She needs to remember her calendar a bit better.

"Apparently, his parents invested some money they earned into some technological companies at the right time and became very rich."

Angela waits to hear the next question as Addison crosses his arms across his chest. He begins to look down at the floor. Angela wonders why he is acting odd. This is not Addie.

"Addie, I know you have other questions you want answered. Why are you not asking them?"

Without changing his gaze on the floor, Addison replies, "I am simply attempting to figure out the validity of something I heard about his parents and their money. I believe it to be bad gossip created from jealousy. With what you just told me, it is more than likely just that."

"What did you hear, Addie?"

Addison leans forward, places his elbows on his knees and clasps his hands together. Biting his lips together and shaking his head a bit, he takes his gaze off of the floor and states, "I heard they were a working class couple with one child. They kept very quiet about home life and people rarely saw the child, which is not really weird. However, someone swears the couple use to take pictures of him and sell them."

"What is wrong with that? They liked photography or wanted Nicholas to be a model. Perhaps, they did use that money for the investments. Who cares?"

Addison shakes his head and states, "No, you are not understanding what I attempted to tell you. The individual that told me swears the photographs were child pornography. I attempted to convince him standards back then were not seen as they are now and the couple may not have thought of it as pornographic. However, he swore they thought of it as pornographic and sold the images to pedophiles."

Angela sees the distress in Addison's face. Apparently, he is having trouble casting what he was told as a lie. Angela looks away for a moment to think on what he told her. She knows none of it should matter for his parents are dead and neither her nor Addie have an extremely strong connection with Nicholas. Yet, the moment seems a bit different than a newscaster stating it. This is someone they both met, enjoyed his company and want to know more about.

"Addie, I say we ignore what was said and continue our interactions with Nicholas. He does a lot of good with his foundations. If they did that to him, I hope they burn in Hell as we speak. He should not suffer in any way for it."

Addie shakes his head and states, "No, he should not be seen as anything than a normal human being. If or if not suffering from sick parents, he seems to live a good life and contributes to good causes. It is just when you told me about the investing, I simply could not help wonder if the story was true."

Angela nods and states, "Would you like a glass of wine? I know I need more."

Addie laughs and replies, "No, Angela, I am through interrupting your day. I need to go home and relax as well. Have a wonderful evening."

"You as well."

Angela watches Addie rise and walk out of the apartment. She hopes what she heard is truly just lies created by jealous people. Thinking any child of suffering from child pornography rips her heart to shreds.

She rises off the couch and walks over to fill her wine glass. She thinks she will watch a movie to take her mind off this conversation. She does not regret talking about it. She simply does not want to continue thinking about it and a good movie shall easily solve the issue.

As she turns to go pick out a movie, she realizes she forgot to tell Addie the most important thing about that meal. He is going to kill her when he finds out she has Nicholas's personal contact information. Oh well, perhaps the next time they talk.

Chapter 11

NICHOLAS SITS IN THE kitchen and watches Peter garnish their meal. He wonders how long it took Peter to learn how to do such splendor. His parents never taught him anything like it. Even though he knows Peter's parents cooked better than his parents and taught Peter, he is also aware the knowledge held by Peter's parents was not to the extent Peter knows and demonstrates. Obviously, the man spent time learning the craft in various ways and locations other than home.

As Peter places the plate in front of him and sits down, Nicholas states, "Thank you, Peter. Looks wonderful."

"Your welcome."

Nicholas takes a bite and feels the flavor melt within his mouth. Moments like this make him desire to forget standards and just gobble it all down. However, doing such will be short lived. So, he shall take his time and cherish every bite.

"I am surprised I have not seen more of those ladies whom shared your mid-day meal the other day. You seemed to get along very well with one of them. Did they ditch you?" states Peter with a cocky smile.

"No, Peter, I simply have been busy."

Nicholas watches Peter nod his head and examine his plate as if something new appears. He knows Peter is attempting to get him to talk about Angela. Unfortunately, he does not know why or what is so important about Peter learning about Angela. Is he interested in her? The thought of them together angers him a bit and he is not sure why. He admits he finds her attractive and likes interacting with her. However, he has no ownership over her and obtaining it is not in his plans for life.

"Your obviously curious about Angela. What is it you need to know, Peter? Are you planning on cheating on Macy?"

Peter drops his fork and glares at him. He should have thought before joking about Macy. Peter claims she saves his life from all that is bad. However, Nicholas does not exactly see it same way since Peter works for him and there are many life flaws in choosing to be around him. So, how is she saving him from all that is bad?

"Sorry, I apparently misunderstood your interest."

"Nicholas, your misunderstanding of people's intents is what keeps you alone at night in this huge home. Watching that girl interact with you, it was easy to see she finds you attractive. Yet, you slowly roam around, play games and only talk. Do you ever have a sexual desire?" states Peter as he breaks into laughter.

Nicholas laughs and picks at his plate. He knows Peter is correct. He spends so much time doing for others and never looks into his own needs. Of course, it is not like he was brought up to interact with others on a personal level. Friends were never allowed over and staying at their house was forbidden. The thoughts of having a girlfriend in high school were killed quick by the inability to share time outside of school in any way. He hates the decisions his parents made for him. And creating friendships and romances now, is much harder on him than people think.

"Peter, I do need to talk with you about something concerning Angela. She grew up in a suburb of here. Her brother apparently use to runaway a lot and eventually never came home. Do you recall hearing anything about it?"

Peter takes a drink and then replies, "Our local news generally does not cover the burbs. Once in a while, they cover runaways, but generally only families with money. I knew many a runaway growing up and nothing ever displayed on the news about them. What is his name?"

Nicholas begins to feel stupid. In all the questions he asked about her brother and support he offered, he never bothered to ask for the boy's name.

"I admit a moment of stupidity, Peter. I forgot to ask."

Peter busts into laughter and stomps his foot as he holds onto the counter. With each stomp, Nicholas feels a bit more ignorant.

"Boy, now, I know you need to connect with Angela a bit more. You apparently desired to know her a bit better and help her through a moment. Though, more importantly, your mind stayed on her rather than grabbing a cape and saving the day."

Nicholas laughs and takes a drink.

"I tell you what, Nicholas. You connect with her and get more information. Once you have it, let me know and I will seek out people I know to find you more information. Now, I cannot guarantee I will find anything out. However, I know people who know people who do not want to be known. So, you may be lucky and actually find the boy."

"Man, he is a man now. Well, if he is still alive. It is not like runaways are safe on the streets. He may simply be dead in an unmarked grave."

After stating the possibility of death, Peter stares at him with blank expression. He is not sure why, but he feels as if he just hit the pause button on Peter. Nicholas knows he wants to say something.

"What, Peter?"

"Good Lord, I hoped you were joking."

Nicholas still has no idea what he is talking about. He simply stated the brother is a man's age now and possibly dead. How does that change a conversation?

"Please tell me what you are thinking. I am lost."

"Nicholas, you may have grown up poor at one time. However, I can tell you your poor is not anywhere near my life of poor. The city does not bury bodies for free, which means the homeless do not have graves. Runaways fall into the same category. If the boy died, then his cremated ashes are sitting in a box with a number on it on a shelf waiting with other boxes to be claimed by a family member. Unfortunately, many remain unclaimed because they do not know who they cremated or cannot find any next of kin connections."

Nicholas feels sadness wash over him. He knows Angela does autopsies for the coroner's office. Is it possible her brother's ashes are sitting in her workplace? He imagines she shall hate herself if she finds out he was and she never looked. The death alone will hurt her, but being in a numbered box right in front of her and never taking the time to realize it is her brother is a bit harsher than finding out he is dead.

"Peter, you prove your point very well. I did not think of what the city does with such corpses."

Peter shakes his head and states, "Do not worry on it. The man may very well be alive and living in a home as nice as this one. We do not know yet. I will talk with my people and find out what I can. It may take a bit of time though."

"Perfectly fine. Take all the time you need."

Peter smiles and states, "You must promise me one thing though."

"What?"

"You cannot simply call up Angela and ask her brother's name. I demand you take the girl out for the evening. Eat at a restaurant or see a movie with her before you go asking about the brother."

Nicholas feels his eyes narrow. Does Peter desire to learn the name through bribery? Or, does he desire to create something unimaginable. Well, unimaginable to Nicholas. Peter seems to have a whole different view of the matter.

"And, what is this supposed to do?"

Peter shakes his head and stares up at the ceiling. Nicholas knows it was probably the wrong question to ask.

"I do not know what it will do. I hope it will get you more connected with the girl and get you laid. You need some excitement in your life."

Nicholas chuckles and replies, "Alright, I will take her out to do something, but do not think it guarantees sex. And, if she declines my offer, I will have no choice but to simply ask the name."

Peter throws his hands up and states, "Perfectly understandable. I doubt she will decline though."

Nicholas simply looks at him as a bright smile crosses his face. He knows Peter hopes it will all work out. Hell, he would enjoy it if him and Angela became something. Unfortunately, getting to anything with a female is not as easy as it sounds. And he does not have any idea what he will do if feelings for her develop. His life would change and some of it he cannot see changing for anyone.

Chapter 12

ANGELA STANDS NEXT to the sink and scrubs her hands. She is not looking forward to this autopsy. She never does when they are so little. She feels as a cruel monster when she sees a baby's face and begins to cut. She reminds herself she is not mutilating a beautiful cherub. For she knows if the child is there, then she must complete the work and take sanctity she is either helping convict someone for what they have done or saving an unfortunate person from a wrongful conviction. Or, in some cases, simply explaining to grieving parents why their precious angel is no longer with them.

After walking away from the sink, she begins to dry her hands as Winston enters the room.

"Angela, you will have to wait to begin. Mr. Baker is requesting our presence in the conference room. Apparently, another death has taken place."

Angela shakes her head and squints her eyes as she asks, "Why does another death take authority over my current autopsy? I can do them both. Do we even have access to the new body yet?"

Winston replies, "No, the police are investigating the scene. The body is still there because they have not instructed anyone to get it. Perhaps, there is something very strange with this one as well."

"I guess there is possibly meaning in the interruption. Though I doubt I need to hear anything on the investigation because in performing the autopsy it is not needed. Its my job to review the body and why they died. Nothing other than the body will assist me in doing it."

Winston winces and states, "On a more positive note, we need to stop by the receptionist's desk as well because you have a delivery."

Angela walks towards the door and asks, "What kind of delivery? I did not order anything."

As Angela opens the door to exit, Winston races up behind her and states, "I do not know. She would not tell me, but she said you should like it."

Taking large steps to keep up with Angela, Winston wonders if Nicholas sent Angela something. She knows it is more than likely something from Addison. However, to make the day a bit more cheery, she prays it is from Nicholas.

Angela reaches the reception desk and asks, "Where is my delivery? I was almost commanded to like it."

The receptionist's eyes widen in disbelief of her behavior, but Angela does not care. No one shall assume they know her mind and tell others what she will or will not like. Her day is interrupted already from the way she expected it to go. She hates that. Yet, she hates people thinking they know her thoughts even more.

The receptionist simply reaches behind her and takes a white rose with a card attached off of her shelf. With calmer eyes and a smile, she hands it to Angela.

Angela's hands begin to slightly shake as she looks down at the rose. She has no idea who sent the rose. She knows the card will simply tell her, but she does not desire to be disappointed. She knows it is probably from Addie, but she wishes it to be from the wonderful looking Nicholas. With the mood she is in right now, she needs it to be from Nicholas.

"Well, are you not going to open it?"

Angela tenses up from hearing a recognizable male voice. She is not familiar with it, but she knows she heard it before. She looks to Winston and sees a shocked woman. Quickly turning to see who exactly stated the question, Angela feels a need for a gun. She cannot believe he is here.

Angela turns to the receptionist and states, "Call the police. This is man is harassing me and I feel threatened."

Javier Alexander quickly rushes to the counter and states, "Do not call anyone. I am here for a meeting."

"Oh, I seriously doubt that. This man confronted Winston and I in the mall in attempt to get us to leave with him. Now, he has found us at our work."

The receptionist looks to Javier and asks, "What is your name and whom are you meeting?"

"My name is Javier Alexander. I am meeting with Mr. Baker and two other individuals."

Winston taps on Angela's arm and whispers, "I did not tell anyone about this meeting other than you. Mr. Baker did state another person shall partake in the meeting."

As the receptionist calls Mr. Baker, Angela asks, "Why are you meeting with Mr. Baker?"

Javier loudly exhales and then turns towards her. She can tell he is extremely frustrated. However, he should think on how she feels.

"I am the lead detective on a case and need to meet with the people performing the autopsies. Are you satisfied? If so, return to whatever hole you randomly crawl out of because I am through with my attempt to know you."

Angela stares at him in disbelief. She cannot understand the irony of the situation. The work she performs assists someone she deems a threat to her and Winston. She is on her way to a meeting about her work that requires her to interact with the person she deems a threat. And, if his proclamation is correct, his job is society's security and he prefers she simply disappear. She has no clue how to perceive this moment from a work standpoint nor correct the mistakes of it on a personal level. The moments with this man are apparently a huge mess and simply are about to get worse when he realizes he is here to talk with her and Winston as well.

"Javier, welcome to the coroner's office." states Mr. Baker as he walks past Angela to shake Javier's hand.

Angela desires to sink into the ground as Mr. Baker turns to her and Winston.

"Let me introduce you to the other people you wish to speak to about your case."

Angela watches Javier's jaw drop upon realizing Mr. Baker intends to introduce him to her and Winston. Angela feels as if she is about to puke.

It is as if her body just dropped to Hell and is roasting as Javier looks past her and Winston in search of people Mr. Baker desires to introduce.

Mr. Baker smiles wide and states, "This is Angela Summers. She performs the autopsies. And next to her is Winston Howell. She listens to Angela's recordings of the autopsies and writes the reports Angela signs off on. Ladies, this is Dectective Javier Alexander. He is handling the serial murderer case."

Angela views Javier's clenched jaw and prays he does not explode. If he wishes another person take over the autopsies, she really does not take offense to it. However, Winston may be disappointed because it will limit their lunchroom talks.

"Hello, ladies. Lets put this nonsense behind us and focus on the reason I am here." states Javier.

Angela knows Javier is simply attempting to be polite. She begins to tense when Mr. Baker looks to her and Winston as if they suddenly grew something out of their heads.

"Is there something I am missing here?" asks Mr. Baker.

Before Angela can think of a reply, Winston steps in and states, "No, Mr. Baker. Mr. Alexander simply attempted to dine with us this past weekend and our lack of knowing him caused us to turn him down. And with his appearance here today, Angela thought we were in danger. A small misunderstanding that is really simply caused by the murders taking place."

Angela watches Mr. Baker grin as he states, "Well, I can see the confusion in all that. These ladies as well as the rest of society should remain vigilant and protect themselves when necessary. I am sure you can understand their viewpoint on the situations, Mr. Alexander."

"Please call me Javier." states Javier as he nods.

Angela may be paranoid, but she believes he was happier looking at Winston when saying that than when gaze drifted to her. She really wants to know who sent the rose, but the tragedy of this morning tells her to wait. The rose may be the only thing to perk her spirit after today.

Desiring to progress to the true intention of them talking to one another, Mr. Baker states, "Ok, now we all know each other, lets go to the boardroom and discuss what Javier wants us to know."

Mr. Baker begins walking and Javier simply follows. Angela turns to Winston.

"Angela, you cannot blame him for his actions this morning."

Angela shakes her head and states, "I am not. I simply wish this day to end."

As they begin walking, Winston states, "Well, are you going to open the card to see who sent the rose?"

"No, I am going to wait until after this meeting."

Winston giggles and tugs Angela to walk a faster pace. She does not mind. She simply wishes to get through this moment without looking like a total idiot.

Chapter 13

UNDER A CLOUDY SKY, Addison quickly enters his employer's building. He really doubts he shall stay at his desk today because the dull personalities often surrounding his desk are not his desire. He simply wants to retrieve some information in his desk, research some things, call a few people to make some connections and leave. He can write the article from home.

After quickly walking down the hall and into the writing room, he is in a bit of shock. Mr. Nicholas Payne is seated in the chair next to his desk. What on earth causes this to happen?

Addison rushes over to his chair and takes a seat. Rather than provoke conversation, he simply leans back and looks at Nicholas. Mr. Payne apparently has an agenda. So, Addison shall let him speak and look upon him. He does not intend it to be sexual in any way. However, admiring a male specimen such as Nicholas Payne is always a blessing.

Appearing to find discomfort, Nicholas Payne clears his throat and states, "I imagine you wonder why I am here."

Addison desires to laugh at his nervous grin. He looks quickly around the room to see who in the room is watching them. With certain people around, he makes it a point to limit the topic of conversations. Thankfully, he is clear of busy bodies today.

"The moment is a bit odd and unique." states Addison with a smile.

Nicholas nods and replies, "Yes, it is and I am the one creating it because I need your assistance. You have information I need."

Addison laughs loudly and various heads turn his direction. He must take to writing a diary to record this moment of the sexy, rich Nicholas Payne desiring his knowledge. He doubts the moment shall ever happen again and historical documentation shall work wonders for his image of life after he passes away. Heaven knows most of the other moments of his life do not portray a wonderful portrait.

"I cannot imagine you needing information I have hidden away. Yet, I am willing to partake this adventure with you. What can I tell you?"

Nicholas fidgets in his seat and leans forward.

"I decided to take an approach towards something today and find myself lacking information. I am sure you are aware of recent interactions with your friend, Angela, and I. Today, I sent a white rose to Angela's work with a card asking if she shall like to have dinner with me."

"Oh dear, no!"

Nicholas sits up quickly and stares at Addison as he asks, "What? Did I do something terrible? Is she with someone else?"

Addison shakes his head and states, "No, you broke some of Angela's personal rules."

"She has rules?"

After Nicholas calms a bit, Addison smiles and replies, "Just little odd ones when it comes to associating with others. I can tell you some of them. I would state them all, but I do not believe she has thought of them all yet. Unfortunately, I am the sole record keeper of her mental rules of association, which is why people do not associate with her. Each time someone attempts to do so, a rule seems to spark from her head into the air."

Addison sees Nicholas's scowl and wonders if he should have refrained from tossing his hands up to emphasize "into the air."

"Nicholas, please do not become disenchanted because I mention a flaw I find personally annoying. She oddly has some connection with you she likes."

Watching Nicholas smile, Addison knows the man is back on the hook and its time to reel him into Angela's world.

"The rule you crossed is very simple. Well, there are two actually. The first one is the crossing of a workplace and personal life. She just does not allow it. I often defy the rule, but I do not suggest others to do it. She gets a bit pissy when you do."

Nicholas asks, "Does she like to keep distance because of her type of work? I imagine it is very difficult to perform autopsies on those you know. Of course, under certain circumstances, you could find solace in knowing the cause of death. Also, there is a possibility you would bring comfort to others you know or save a living friend from charges. There are circumstances I think you can find comfort in performing the autopsies."

Addison continues to look at him and blink in disbelief of this guy's random dissertation of Angela's work. Is he as nerdy as she?

"Nicholas, stay on subject. The subject is her mental flaws, not her work." replies Addison. "She likes to keep distance because her father taught her and her brother home life and work do not mingle. His theory is work and family conflict each other in purpose of existing unless you operate a family business, such as a farm. By sending the flower to her work, you crossed the line drawn between the two."

Nicholas replies, "I had no other choice. I do not know where she lives."

Addison shakes his head and states, "Do not state excuses. She hates excuses. Well, she hates my excuses. I am not too sure about others because I have yet to see anyone's moment of using excuses in attempt to get her to understand their thought in doing something. Moreover, you should make a personal effort rather than hiding behind a flower. Yes, its pretty, but you are attempting to obtain a personal connection between you and her. The flower has nothing to do with the scenario nor the card."

"This shall sound a bit odd, but I really have trouble connecting with others."

Addison watches as Nicholas begins to look around the room. He professionally so desires to find the truth about Nicholas's past and write a story. However, the questions are very delicate and their location is not a good location for such topics. So, he will need to suck up his desire for Angela's sake.

"Nicholas, I shall tell you something and you cannot mention a word to Angela about it. She is interested in you. I knew it at the event you hosted and it has not diminished. Relax and get to know the girl."

Nicholas smiles and asks, "What is the second rule?"

Addison sighs and states, "The card, you dumcoff. Why else would I mention personal effort? She does not like notes, letters, emails, or any texts when communicating on a personal level. She likes personal interactions to be personal."

Nicholas takes a deep breath and states, "Okay, I think I understand what I need to do. I just need you to answer a question, which is the reason I came here."

"The question is?"

"What type of food does she like? I plan to take her to a restaurant because I do not want her to feel stressed about intimacy by having my chef make us a dinner at my home."

"Just take her to Cardone's. Best food in town and a diverse menu with some unique meals."

Nicholas nods and smiles. Addison cannot believe the man came to his work to ask a question about where to eat. He surely has other's capable of making the suggestion.

"Addison, you saved me and hope to see more of you. Thank you!" states Nicholas as he rises and holds out his hand.

Addison shakes his hand and replies, "Your welcome."

He watches Nicholas walk away. The back view is as nice as the front. And, by the rise in volume of people talking, he is sure others are admiring it as well. Or, simply questioning how Addison made connections with the guy. Because I am brilliant, bitches!

Chapter 14

AS A DRIZZLE OF RAIN falls on the window, Angela listens to the soft tones playing from her stereo. She closes her eyes and rests her head on the back of the couch. She believes today is truly a day to throw away.

The moments of the day keep running through her mind and she desires to blame someone. Unfortunately, she feels all others in the situation choose to blame her. Yet, she truly believes Javier is at fault for a lot of the situation. He should have identified himself in the mall as working for the police department. She would have asked for verification of course, but it still would have calmed the moment and kept her actions of today from occurring. And, perhaps, she and Winston may have decided to join him if he had introduced himself properly.

Instead, he simply acted as a creep roaming the mall for personal enjoyment at other people's expense. He created the whole unsavory moment. Though acting so did cause her to obtain a wonderful meal with Nicholas Payne, which could say a positive thing for Javier. However, she does not feel he deserves credit for the wonderful afternoon. Only one person deserves credit for it. Nicholas...

Thinking of him, Angela remembers she forgot to open the card attached to the rose. She simply came home and placed it on the kitchen counter. She must remind herself the arrival of the rose at the same time of Javier does not mean the rose is from Nicholas. Addie may have sent it. The only way to know is if she looks. She opens her eyes and rises off the couch.

As she walks to the kitchen, she gets nervous. What if she allowed her imagination to run wild and its not from Nicholas? What if it is from someone that simply appreciates her work?

She laughs at the absurdity of the thought as she picks the flower up and opens the envelope. She pulls out the card and walks away before looking at it. She knows she is acting like a cat scared of its own shadow, but she prefers to sit down to read it. It is really a safety measure on mentality if you think about it. If the rose is from Nicholas, she shall be safe if she passes out from the wonderful excitement. If it is from someone else, then she can toss it on the table and begin relaxing again.

She sits down on the couch and remains hesitant. She will be so disappointed if it is not from Nicholas. After a deep breath, she looks down at the card and scans to the bottom to see who it is from.

Her hand covers her mouth when she realizes it is from Nicholas. She quickly jumps to the top of the card and begins reading. Realizing he is asking her out to dinner, her hand drops from her mouth as her eyes begin to bulge and her jaw drops. At the end, she sees he left his phone number on the card as well as the adorable notation "in case you cannot find my card". Like she would really forget!

With the excitement built within her, Angela desires to jump up and tell the world. Well, not the world, but Addison and Winston will work. However, that would be stupid since she has yet to secure the dinner by calling him. She thrusts her feet up and down while screaming "yes" to release some of the excitement before calling him. She does not desire to seem too overzealous when speaking with Nicholas.

Angela exhales deeply and picks up the phone to begin dialing. She prays the phone does not ring continuously before being directed to voicemail.

"Hello." answers Nicholas.

Angela loves the sound of his voice over the phone. The strong tone reminds her of his wonderful body.

"Hello, Nicholas. This is Angela."

She knows she should probably say more, but she does not desire to control the conversation. If his desire is to woo her into submission, then she is all for it. Who is she kidding! If he desires her to dominate it all, she will.

"Angela, I am glad you called. I take it you received the flower today. I want to apologize for sending it to your work. I simply could not think of another way to reach you. When I gave you my card, I should have thought to ask for your phone number."

Angela begins to melt from his thoughtfulness. She does not know many men willing to apologize for sending gifts.

"There is no need to apologize, Nicholas. Your gift was a refreshing surprise after a rather harsh day. I am thankful you sent it."

Angela hopes he hears her smile in her voice. God knows it is ear to ear at this moment. She is so excited, jumping in the car and going to his place at this exact moment sounds wonderful. If only he would ask her to do so!

"I shall take a risk and break this awkward moment. Will you join me for dinner Saturday night?" asks Nicholas.

"Yes."

Angela knows she should say more, but she simply cannot think of what to say. She feels like a love stricken school girl.

"Wonderful, I will pick you up at seven. Well, if it is alright with you? I know some people prefer separate vehicles."

Angela giggles and replies, "I trust you enough. You may pick me up. My address is 1515 Sunnycove Lane."

After a brief silence, Nicholas replies, "Wonderful! Oh, I want to tell you I intend to take you to Cardone's simply because I do not want you to over or under dress and feel uncomfortable. Unless you have a problem with the place? I have yet to experience it."

"I have not either. I hear the place is nice. Great food without requiring you to wear a major fashion designer. Though I shall dress better than dinner at Long Horn Steakhouse. So, you best be prepared!" states Angela with a laugh.

"Oh, I shall!"

The faint growl in the last statement makes her desire more. Angela waits and wonders if he will carry on the conversation.

"Well, Angela, I am actually on my way to something. I love you called and shall most definitely see you on Saturday. However, I must go."

"Not an issue, Nicholas. I shall see you Saturday. Have a wonderful evening."

"You as well!"

Angela ends the call and falls back on the couch. She finds it remarkable to feel so comfortable with him. She does not know why she does. Her excitement diminished a bit after hanging up. Though she can only tell because she no longer feels a need to shout to the world about the rose from Nicholas. She will happily tell others, but this moment is hers. And, she intends to savior it.

Chapter 15

ANGELA LOOKS AROUND the lobby as she travels to her workplace. Everyone seems to partake in their normal routine. She finds the view unfortunate since she sees the world as slightly changed after her conversation with Nicholas. All those around her seem to not notice, but she does not care. She has something to look forward to and they are not a part of it.

Having walked to the transcriptionists' room, she notices Winston at her desk about to place her headphones on. Angela increases her step and taps her on the shoulder. Winston places her headphones down and looks to Angela.

With all the story to tell, Angela decides to lean up against the wall next to the desk. She knows she may be here a bit.

"Wow, aren't you full of energy today? Spill it! Was the flower from Addison or Nicholas?" states Winston.

Angela feels the large smile form across her face. Its a good thing she does not need to lie. She would not be able to convince anyone of anything at this moment.

"The wonderful flower was from Nicholas. The card was him requesting a date."

"No way!" exclaims Winston with mouth agape.

"Yes, we shall have dinner Saturday evening. The wonderful Nicholas shall pick me up and take me to Cardone's, which will be the first time there for both of us."

"Wow! I wish I had your life. We go to the meeting from Hell and you are compensated with a rich man attempting to sweep you off your feet. I went home to my dog. Now, do not get me wrong. I love Brutus. However, a man's attractive warm body is much better to curl up with after a trying day."

Angela looks away. She does not intend for her happiness to cause sadness for another. And to take the conversation to a chipper mood, she is not sure how to reply.

"Now, do not analyze my sadness as unhappiness you brought to me. See it as some man's failure to recognize me as a great person to be with. Do the woman thing. Blame men!" jokes Winston.

Angela laughs and pulls a nearby chair to her. She sits down to chat a bit more. Never has she done this in the past and she does not intend to make it a habit. She simply desires to connect with Winston, which considering her rules is very odd.

"Moreover, blame the man who brought us the horrible meeting. I am willing to take blame for it starting badly. However, he needs to take blame for not giving more identity when we met and attempting to take control of how we work."

Winston nods and replies, "Very true! Though I can understand his frustration and why he called the meeting. With his boss contacting the FBI for assistance, he wants to make sure everything is done properly."

Angela rolls her eyes and states, "The FBI will see an autopsy as an autopsy. Nothing in procedure of one changes. We look at everything. I understand he wants to make sure everything is accurate and documented properly. However, he has yet to see anything appearing improper from us. So why bother making a fire?"

"Because he wants to blow miserable nothings in our ears!" jokes Winston.

They burst into laughter.

"Perhaps I can direct him towards Addison. He blows misery at him and a match shall break out. It would definitely be a battle where people shall desire to wage money on a winner."

"How did Addison take your receiving the flower and card? I am sure he is jealous beyond belief."

Angela quickly looks away as she states, "I have not told Addison yet. You are actually the first person I told."

Wide-eyed and smirking, Winston looks around the room. Angela is sure she is shocked to hear such a statement from her.

"I simply did not tell him yet because I was basking in the pleasure of Nicholas asking me. I did not feel a desire to rush out and tell the world. I made it my own personal joy."

Winston nods and replies, "You should make it your personal pleasure. The moment is for you and Nicholas. Addison will just cause turmoil and unwanted publicity once he decides to write a story on it."

Angela shakes her head and states, "No, I think Addison shall avoid personal stories of Nicholas for a bit. After the conversation he and I had, I think Addison was scared off of investigating Nicholas's life. Some shocking things may have occurred and Addie does not care to hear about it."

Angela waves to a co-worker in the distance as Winston looks upon her. She knows Winston wants her to continue. However, their environment is not really suitable for conversation about what did or did not occur in Nicholas's past. What environment it would be acceptable is beyond her knowledge, but here a major red flag is thrown.

"So, I take it you are not going to tell me about that conversation. Is it because you do not desire bad thoughts of Nicholas? Or, do you not trust me?"

"No, Winston, nothing such as that. Addie simply heard some rumors about Nicholas's parents that paint an abusive childhood. I can tell you more of the conversation. However, at work, is the wrong place to discuss it because of what the rumor states. Victims in such cases would not desire anyone to hear about it."

"If it is that bad, I do not want to hear it at all. Just not my kind of thing to talk about. Atrocities against children is disgusting and I have seen enough of it." states Winston as she picks up her headset.

"Really? You never told me you were abused." replies Angela.

Winston roles her eyes and states, "My parents abused me with obsessive hugs. I am talking about abuse through neighborhoods I lived, news stories and the transcriptions of abuse victims I complete. You do not need to go far to hear about adults attacking the weak."

Angela feels her happiness lower a bit. She guesses she needs to put more thought into conversation instead of blurting things out.

"I am sorry for assuming you talked about yourself. What you say is very true. Perhaps we can convince this serial killer to realize people such as that are good targets." jokes Angela.

Angela watches Winston cross her self before she states, "Dear Lord, please forgive us for calling for death of abusers."

Angela stares at her and wonders if this conversation can get more odd.

Winston looks to her and states, "I believe all have a right to life and calling for murder is sinful."

Angela is a bit shocked by the proclamation. Winston generally is very vocal on wishing retaliation on things she does not appreciate.

Noticing the odd expression, Winston states, "I worry the killer will make mistakes or take a simple punishment as abuse. Javier told me the main reason why they are contacting FBI for help is because the motive seems odd. Oh, by the way, you will have another body coming in today or tomorrow. The next victim was found. Well, what they think is the next victim. Javier is not sure if it is or if a copycat is acting out."

Hearing Javier's name sends Angela into a moment of annoyance. Even more hateful is the fact Winston apparently had conversation with him she was not aware of taking place. She knows it is childish. However, she is finally connecting with Winston on a personal level and Javier is working his way in as well. Playground is getting a bit crowded for her taste.

"Winston, I really should go. I will chat at lunch more. Have a good day!"

As Winston nods and puts on her headset, Angela walks away. She wants to be rid of Javier and his mass murderer. They are the only two things she does not appreciate about her life at this moment. Well, in a brief thought of her life. If she looked in detail and made a list, she is sure more negative things will stand out. However, she hates negative things and really does not care to keep a list of them.

Now thanks to that conversation, to get rid of this negativity before Saturday, she is going to have to talk with Addie about all of it. Oh well, perhaps the news of Nicholas will help calm Addie and keep him from writing a news story about the officer she cannot stand. Though she is sure she will have to bite her tongue several times to keep Addie from flying into brilliant ideas that are not so brilliant. Oh well, just another conversation with Addison.

Chapter 16

SITTING IN A QUIET room with only the sound of typing, Nicholas sits and waits for his attorney to speak with him. Moments like this he feels as if time is totally wasted. Obviously, he is not Fred's only client nor desires to be the only one paying the man. He simply wishes moments like this did not happen.

The door to Fred's office opens and Fred steps out. He looks briefly at his paralegal and states, "I am going to need the Cumbers paperwork by this evening. She is really pushing to close the deal and fears we will delay it. Whatever gave her that idea I do not know."

"Yes, sir."

Fred motions for Nicholas to join him in his office. He rises and walks in while Fred holds the door open. As he moves towards the chair to sit down, he hears the door close. He takes a seat and asks, "Do you feel a walk through shall take place soon? I know they have been working hard on the improvements and you hired a company to assist with security measures."

He watches Fred sit down behind his desk.

"A walk through shall take place in about two weeks. They ran into some water issues that delayed the remodeling. However, it is not why I asked you here today."

Nicholas's brow scrunches a bit for he was not expecting any new conversation. The only work going on is the boys' home. He is still searching for a location of the girls' home after deciding against the initial property because of a rat infestation.

"What do you desire to discuss?"

Nicholas watches him pull a file out of his desk and lay it down. The file is not thick. So, apparently, it is a simple matter to discuss.

"There are two matters of interest. The first deals with the boys' home. A security company is offering a professional security team to monitor everything onsite." states Fred as he taps on the folder. "I know you do not desire to make the place feel as a jail. However, I have ideas on how we can avoid that representation."

Nicholas sits back and thinks on the issue. Obviously, a top security team is a wonderful idea to ensure safety. Yet, he is not sure about trusting adults to treat emancipated kids with respect. Many simply view the kids as children refusing to behave.

"As you know, I feel dictatorship is not to exist in this home. With a counselor on duty at all times, I feel the boys shall have proper direction. The security team's point of existence is as simple as securing the building from intruders. What type of monitoring are they offering?"

Fred replies, "Well, they want to keep their security guys on site, which means they are the first thing seen on entry."

Nicholas feels his body tense a bit. He knows it is not necessarily a bad thing to see upon arrival. However, he does not know how the boys will deem it.

"Before you explode, Nicholas, realize the security company does not desire staff interaction with the boys other than a nod with a smile or can I help you with that package. I had a serious discussion with them. They are fully aware the security staff will operate as doormen without opening the door. They will simply monitor who is going in and out while watching the video monitors."

Nicholas nods and asks, "What is the cost? Does it increase the rent the boys will have to pay?"

Fred smiles and replies, "No, the cost is still under the threshold. I told you when discussing the design you allotted a huge amount to security for no reason."

"Okay. Where do I need to sign?"

Fred opens the folder and turns it so Nicholas can see the contract. As he is reading it, Fred hands him a pen.

Fred states, "You simply need to initial mid-page and sign at the bottom."

Nicholas does as he is told and closes the folder. After capping the pen, he pushes everything back to Fred.

"Now, the other issue I want to discuss is a crazy rumor I heard. I hear you are romantically involved with someone."

Nicholas's eyes widen. He cannot imagine how Fred heard anything like that. He has yet to take Angela out on a date and he has been home at night by himself. Perhaps she mentioned something to someone.

"I am not sure why you hear such a thing. I have asked someone on a date, but we have yet to go out."

Fred states, "Okay, I am understanding a bit more. Apparently, jealousy or mistrust causes the rumor. Who are you seeing? I can run a check on her and squash the rumors."

Nicholas feels confused on such a statement. Rumors always take place. The only way to kill them is for people to stop talking.

"Fred, what do you mean run a check on her? This is my personal life. I am not creating a business deal with her."

Fred shakes his head and states, "No, Nicholas, it is not a business deal. However, some women do think of it as such. They target men with money. I simply desire to protect you from such a person."

Nicholas looks to the floor as he thinks. He cannot imagine Angela looking at him for money. If he allows Fred to intrude on her life, then he definitely will never see her again. He cannot imagine anyone desiring to be around him with Fred investigating everyone. He almost wants to laugh at the absurdity of it. He often wished someone would see into his life when he was younger. No one ever did. Of course, they do not now either. Now, the only thing people generally see are either his money or his charitable work. He knows his life now would confuse some upon learning his actions, but many of them would understand him a bit more.

"No, Fred, I choose to keep my personal life private. And, if you desire to keep me as a client, then you will not ask such questions again. You have helped me in the past in finding information on people and you may in the future. However, it is for me to decide upon who and why, not for you to suggest people."

Fred's lips crawl into his mouth as he thinks of a reply. Nicholas does not care to hear any arguments on the matter. He demands control over his life. He fought hard to obtain it and refuses to allow alteration.

"I am sorry, Nicholas. I simply felt you may desire to know more about someone before getting involved."

Nicholas shakes his head as he stands.

"Are we done then? I have a few things I need to do today."

Nicholas watches Fred nod and turns to walk out. Without pausing or acknowledging his intent to depart, he leaves the office. The paralegal looks his way as he walks past her and ignores her existence.

He is frustrated at Fred's assumption of Angela. True, he does not know everything about her. However, it is for him to find out more about her, not read in a report. And, he intends to do just that.

Chapter 17

AS MUSICIANS PLAY CLASSICAL music on the other side of the restaurant, Angela takes a bite of her meal. She quietly chews and wonders if conversation will strike up again. Nicholas's arrival to pick her up went very smooth and conversation was easy. She could tell he was impressed with how she looks when she opened the door. His gaze went from cordial happiness to sexual admiration in a matter of seconds. To cover his attraction, he began a short conversation, but she did not mind.

"The food is not too spicy, is it? I heard the chef sometimes gets very flamboyant with spice." asks Nicholas.

Angela takes a sip of wine and as she smiles states, "No, it is perfectly fine. Did your chef tell you about the spices?"

"No, just someone I had a conversation with about this place."

As they wait for dessert, she wonders what conversation shall arise. So far, they simply chatted about her brother and childhood. She knows she really does not have too much to tell him about life now, but she is sure he does. However, she does not desire to scare him away by asking a trillion questions about his lifestyle.

"So, tell me about your work. I know you and Winston work the same place, but is it the same department or just lunch buddies?"

Angela takes another sip of wine and then explains, "We work together in a way. I perform the autopsies and she writes the reports from my dictation."

"Oh, so you operate like a tag team."

Angela giggles and replies, "No...well, recently yes. Generally, the dictation is done by anyone in her department. However, with the recent murders, I am assigned to complete all the autopsies of possible victims and she is the only one allowed to create the reports for me to sign off on."

A stone cold expression crosses his face as he asks, "Why do they limit it to just you two?"

The expression she sees is so odd. He seems as if something may bother him, but something not really important at all. There is no happiness, curiosity, anger or even a sign of sadness. Angela is not sure if he is upset or simply curious and asking questions he really does not like. Perhaps discussing the murders upset him a bit.

As the waiter places the dessert in front of them, Angela replies, "We did the report on the first victim. And once another appeared, the police asked us to be the only ones to perform them because it appeared to be a serial killer and they want to keep the details out of the press."

A smile crosses his face as she takes a bite of chocolate cheesecake. She relaxes a bit more. She is sure talking about autopsies is not his desire. Yet, he does desire to know more about her work and she is willing to admit most of her life revolves around her work.

"And Nicholas, you will not believe who is in charge of the investigation."

His smile becomes wider and taunting. She definitely is on the right track to getting the discussion on a happier level.

"Who?" asks Nicholas.

"Javier Alexander. You may not remember him as well as I do. He is the man you saved Winston and I from at the mall."

A loud, robust laughter takes over Nicholas. People at several nearby tables look at them. She simply smiles at the other patrons and giggles as Nicholas takes a drink of wine to calm his laughter.

"Mr. Alexander apparently is not too keen on how to properly invite a woman to dine with him. How did he react on finding out your and Winston's role in his investigation?"

"Well, at first, I thought he was stalking us when he showed up at our workplace and I asked the receptionist to call the police. He quickly told her not to because he was there for a meeting. Upon confirmation of who he was and why he was there, he seemed a bit aggravated on finding out our roles."

As he works at eating his dessert, Angela debates on telling him more. Obviously, she cannot tell him about her findings on the victims, but talking about the investigator does not violate anything.

As he takes another sip of his wine, Angela states, "Needless to say, the meeting after the introduction was rather uncomfortable, which increased my stress. However, I was given a wonderful release from it all."

Nicholas gives her an inquisitive stare as she remains quiet.

"Really? How and who? Should I take a defensive approach with the guy?" asks Nicholas with a seductive look that has her desiring much more..

Angela smiles and replies, "No, I do not believe a defense is necessary. I simply received a rose with a request for dining together."

As the waiter places the bill on the table, Angela and Nicholas look into each other's eyes. She feels her body warm as the room seems to disappear around them. The moment seems as if she is standing close to him and awaiting a kiss. She feels as if they are deciding who shall take the bold move of breaking from the other simply to take the moment to another level of seduction.

"Proud to assist you once again." states Nicholas.

Nicholas breaks the heated gaze and takes out a card to pay for the meal. As he slides the card into the holder, Angela tries to think of what to talk about. She really wants back in the moment they just had, but definitely better revisited later tonight.

As the waiter takes the payment away, Nicholas asks, "Do you feel you can obtain a better work stance with Mr. Alexander?

Obviously, you will have interaction of some sort with one another. However, it should not have to be a stressful moment every time."

"Actually, I am not sure how much longer he will be in charge of the investigation. The chief of police has requested assistance from the FBI. I am sure they will probably take control of it all."

"Why do you think they will take control? If the chief only requested assistance, they should do just that."

Angela is taken a bit off-guard by the tone of his voice. There is a bit of anger in it.

"Well, I cannot go into details of the victims, but evidence does point to a serial killer. Our city has never experienced anything like it and I doubt the police force has experience investigating it."

The waiter brings back Nicholas's card and he places it back in his wallet after signing. He then looks to her and asks, "Are you ready to depart?"

Since he asks with his wonderful smile, Angela simply nods and rises. As she pushes her chair in, he stands beside her and offers his arm to escort her out. She walks with him as she thinks of how to get back to a happy conversation. She wants him in a positive mind when offering him to enter her home rather than simply return home. She still wants to leave the sexual advances up to him. However, he is more likely to make them in her home rather than a car. He is too classy to begin in the car and she intends to discover more of him.

Chapter 18

JAVIER SITS AT HIS desk and reviews tasks listed on his calendar. The list is long, but he really cannot be held responsible for it expanding. Most of the tasks rely on waiting for someone else to do their job. If he could do the autopsies or lab results, then the tasls would already be done. Unfortunately, he is waiting on an autopsy report from the witch he attempted to have dinner with on a bored day.

He is still unsure of how a woman can be so attractive, authoritative and unable to associate with other people. She must lead a very lonely life.

"Javier, here is the autopsy report and additional evidence." explains his partner, Steve, as he places a box on his desk.

Javier looks at the box and worries he will spend days looking through evidence. He is happy to have the evidence, but how many will the guy murder while he spends his time looking all of it over for small details.

"Is the entire box full of new evidence? I saw the victim before the autopsy. She did not appear in too terrible condition other than pictures nailed into her body."

Steve shakes his head and jokingly replies, "No, it is not full, but all is new evidence. Just a lot of pictures, articles of clothing and something she was forced to swallow. I did not bother to look to see what it was. I just read the report and know it is Item K."

"Alright, I will look through it all and log it into the evidence room. Does the report share any important information? I assume she died from all the photos attached to her body."

"No, that is not what killed her. Apparently, she died of a drug overdose. Whether she took the drugs willingly or not is the question we need answered. The report states all the photos were attached to her body postmortem, which is why she was not completely soaked in blood when she was found."

Javier is perplexed on this one. He wonders if this is the same killer or if a copy cat appears. The motives of sending a punishment message are the same. However, if a drug overdose killed her, then it simply could be someone finding her body and making sure her victims were released.

"Tell me, Steve, what do you think a person needs to create these punishment messages we keep finding? I like to think someone is unable to perform the murders in their own home before display."

Steve shrugs and pulls up a chair to sit down.

"Nah, I doubt this takes place in a home. If it does, there are not any neighbors around or very deaf ones."

Javier nods and begins looking in the box. Picture upon picture is stacked on the victim's clothing. Each item in its own plastic bag. He mentally tells himself to write a task reminder to talk once again with the victim's victims. After a brief time of freedom, they may remember a bit more and feel safe enough to say it.

"I doubt the drug overdose was willingly. By looking at the photos, I doubt our victim lowered her mentality with drugs. This was her money source. I doubt she restricts operation to get high." states Javier.

Steve politely nods.

"Steve, are you familiar with anything reported at unoccupied industrial buildings? There are several throughout town and most lack neighbors."

Steve shakes his head and replies, "No, I have not heard anything happening recently other than a rich guy moving to town and buying up properties, but he does not rely on just industrial buildings."

Javier wonders who he is talking about. He highly doubts the man is their killer, but the man may have seen something interesting while looking through his purchased buildings.

"Who is this guy? Is he looking to bring more industry to town? Or, does he hope to tear it down and build houses?"

"Neither, Javier. The man is finishing up one building and looking for another to simply help emancipated children. He wants them to be safe and get a fair shot at life."

Javier watches Steve roll his eyes. Apparently, Steve feels assisting a child to be an adult is not worthy of so much money. However, Javier can understand the need and desire to offer assistance. Most emancipated kids have gone through a harsh life with their parents.

"Who is this man? Why did he choose our town? I doubt we offer an extraordinary amount of emancipated children needing assistance."

Steve shakes his head and replies, "His name is Nicholas Payne. He use to live here as a child, but his parents moved away, became rich, died and left it all to Nicholas. If you ask me, I say he is a spoiled rich kid attempting to convince kids they can achieve a better life by not living with nor listening to mom and dad."

Javier is a bit taken aback at Steve's comments. He seems to only look at one side of the whole situation. With emancipated children, the parents generally are not the best to listen to at times. However, it is not worth arguing at this time.

"This guy may be a good resource then. If he has toured buildings and now owns some, he may be able to tell us of any odd things happening around them. I wonder if he will talk with us."

"I do not see why he would not. Though I am sure you can probably expect some fund raising confrontation if you do. He also runs a foundation for kids with incarcerated parents. Held a big fundraising gala for it at his home, which is the gated house outside of town everyone ohs and ahs over."

Javier wonders why he has not heard of the fundraising events until now. Usually, the department is full of talk each time an organization wants to raise money for kids. He imagines it is because of his lack of socialization.

"Oh, I imagine his name will add to the stack of men named Nicholas I do not care to know."

Steve laughs and asks, "Still not forgiving the guy who stole your possible dates?"

Javier smirks and answers, "I simply desired lunch. And no, I just cannot get over it. Especially, after finding out the women work at the Coroner's office and complete the work I need done. I could be having the best investigation of my life right now. The beautiful Angela and I could review her findings, which would cause me to praise her, get a bit closer and have a wonderful night of sex. However, her relationship with a man named Nicholas ruins it all."

Steve shakes his head and replies, "Just let it go. There are other women out there. And, if you become friends with the rich Nicholas, I am sure the choices shall be prime. All women love a rich man."

Javier buries his face in his hands and rubs his eyes. He highly doubts he will become friends with rich Nicholas. He looks back at Steve and replies, "I doubt my luck will ever fall into place where I can just choose a woman. I am too inquisitive about their lives. And women either do not like answerting my questions or they feel I am intruding on their life too much at a rapid pace of time."

Steve shrugs and rises from his chair. As he walks away, Javier wonders why the moment at the mall went so badly. He knows they worried about not knowing him and the murders probably increased the stress. Perhaps he should have identified himself as an officer, but a lot of times that scares women away. Either they do not lead a law abiding life and worry about him joining their life, or they feel the job is too threatening.

Javier decides to think about it another day and begins emptying the box of evidence. He knows with each piece he can be inquisitive as he wants. Perhaps it is why he loves his job so much.

Chapter 19

ANGELA SITS AND BEGINS eating her lunch as talking all around her takes place. Their is an abundance of conversations, but she is not interested in any of them. She simply wishes Winston would arrive. She is dying to tell her about her wonderful date with Nicholas. And, she can use a bit of constructive criticism about how the night went. After talking with Addie on Sunday, she wants a woman's perspective.

Not that she feels Addie was not happy to hear about it, but his responses felt more like a lecture rather than encouragement to develop a relationship with Nicholas. He simply kept asking for details and then telling her what she should or should not have done as if he was telling a child how to properly cook a meal or play an instrument. She has no idea why Addie is so enthralled with them getting connected, but he apparently desires to make it his life mission.

As Winston sits down, Angela smiles wide and waits for her to get situated to eat her lunch. Thankfully, Winston does not appear hungry with the salad she bought. Angela would hate for her friend to choke to death from hearing the crazy date moments. Angela must admit some of it is a little shocking.

"Okay, out with it!" states Winston as she takes her first bite.

Angela takes a sip of her soda and replies, "The wonderful looking Nicholas Payne is an interesting date and every bit a gentleman."

"Did you sleep with him?" Winston asks before shoving lettuce in her mouth.

Angela is a bit taken aback the question is so promptly asked. Would it not be more pleasing to hear about the date prior to inquiring about sex?

"Should a girl tell?"

Angela watches Winston chew harder and wants to laugh. She knows not knowing if she did or did not is driving Winston insane.

"If you do not tell, I just may contact Addie to see what he can find out." states Winston as she lifts her brow to emphasize her demand.

"Oh alright, I will tell you. We did not sleep together. However, it was on my mind and I was willing. He simply desires to be a gentleman and take our connection at a slower pace."

Winston shrugs and replies, "If he desires a strong relationship, then I believe you did the right thing. A bit of a disappointment, but the right thing."

Angela laughs and states, "I agree. However, I must say the goodnight kiss was rather nice. Being close in his arms definitely had my blood boiling."

"So when is the next date?"

Angela shrugs and replies, "I am not sure. I guess I will need to wait a few days to hear from him. Though if I have not heard from him by Thursday, then I will call and invite him to something. I do not know what, but I will find something."

Angela takes a bite of her lunch and looks around the cafeteria. She has not thought about him not calling her until now and it slightly makes her worry. What if the kiss was his way of giving a polite goodbye? Has she created the connection with him in her head?

She looks down at her meal as Winston asks, "Did you talk about anything interesting? What did you learn about him?"

Angela holds back a nervous laugh. She feels a bit stupid for allowing her thoughts to bring her down so quickly. If she simply thought of what they talked about, she would remember what Nicholas promised her and realize he did not blow her off with a kiss.

"We discussed a lot about where we lived and my family. He really did not mention anything about his. More importantly, we discussed my brother and Nicholas is going to use his connections to locate him."

A curious expression crosses Winston's face as she asks, "Is he hiring a private detective?"

"No, he said his chef has many street connections and by giving my brother's name he may be able to find some information on him, such as who he hung out with or where he slept. With that information, I may hire a detective to find more information. I have not done so in the past because I could not find out anything other than the police here are the ones whom usually found him when he ran away."

"They did not give you an address where he was hiding? Where did they find him?"

Angela shakes her head and states, "No, they never found him at a place he was staying. They generally found him stealing from a store and arrested him. After running his information, they would find out he was a runaway and contact my parents."

Angela examines her food as Winston chews her lunch. She hates telling others about her brother's crimes. The thefts were simply an attempt to get money to stay alive. He swore to her none of it was ever for drugs or alcohol. Simply for food or a roof over his head during harsh weather. She knows stealing to live still is not right, but she does understand why he did it.

"I do not want you to think bad things, but do you ever wonder about the possibility your brother may no longer be alive? Your an adult now as is he. Yet, he has not attempted to contact you." inquires Winston.

Angela cringes at the thought. She has thought about it many times. However, she refuses to believe he is dead. He simply wanted a different life than the one his father planned for him. With his creativity and resourcefulness, she cannot imagine him not succeeding at achieving his desires.

"No, Winston, I refuse to believe he may be dead. He simply would not have allowed that to happen. I know it sounds stupid to say, but I have faith in him."

Winston simply nods and continues eating. Angela takes a bite simply to stop talking. She feels so much stress upon her right now. If her brother died, then her parents would have been notified. Well, unless, they were unable to identify the remains. She hates to think he is possibly in this building at this very moment because no body knows who he is. She looks around the room in attempt to take her mind off the matter.

"Did you tell Nicholas about your family's strict rules? If you build a relationship, then at some point he will meet your parents." inquires Winston.

Angela looks to Winston and states, "No, I really did not get into those details. I did not think to add it to the conversation."

Winston nods and continues eating as Angela thinks about the question some more. She truly did not think to tell Nicholas about her father and his rules on life nor her mother's devotion to following them. To Angela, the rules are more of a philosophy to succeed in life. However, she did have to follow all of them while growing up. So to her parents, the rules are not philosophy. She often wonders if they ever thought about deviating from the rules after they lost their son. She knows she often did.

Chapter 20

IAN THOMAS MENTALLY arises from his sleep, but refuses to open his eyes. His head is killing him from last night's drinking. He does not remember leaving the bar nor knows where he currently is. He presumes the whole thing is a story he intends to forget.

With a slight breeze crossing the room, he knows his pants and boxers are gone, but his shirt is still in place. He imagines he hooked up with some harlot and then passed out. The stupid whore apparently did not attempt to get him home, which is a good thing. Nina would have pitched a fit.

Though none of that is his concern right now. Right now, he needs to find out why he feels himself in a sitting position while on his back. His legs are not together. They are up in the air resting on something. And, if it is a couch, then it is either old or cheap because he does not feel cushions under his legs.

Enduring the head pain, Ian slowly opens his eyes to a dark room. He looks around slowly by simply moving his eyes. He sees nothing due to the darkness. He curses and attempts to rise to find a light, but realizes his arms are restrained to whatever his back is laying on. He simply thought some sort of fabric was around his wrists when he awoke. He then realizes he does feel the same fabric and tightness near his ankles. He attempts to move his legs and finds they are also restrained.

He relaxes his body as he attempts to remember more of last night because he knows he needs to get out of this mess. Did some bitch use some S&M on him and leave him in it? He highly doubts it because he never would agree to sexual submission no matter how hot the girl. If his pants were on, he would simply believe Nina's kids did this. Damn brats are always too much trouble.

A light turns on and Ian quickly looks to the right to see who arrives. Once he sees the odd man in a mask covering his eyes as if at a masquerade party walking towards him, Ian begins to worry. He knows it is a man due to lack of tits, but he does not look familiar in any way. He seems of an athletic build and has what Ian thinks are blue eyes. Ian cannot make out his exact hair color due to a hat covering his head. Though he believes it is a dark color because his eyebrows are dark.

"Who the hell are you and why do you have me this way? You best let me go." Ian calmly asks.

The man shakes his head as he stands next to Ian and looks down at him.

"I cannot tell you who I am for I am constantly attempting to figure it out for myself. However, I can explain the why. Though I believe you should examine all you have done so you can realize the why."

Ian squints his eyes and shakes his head in disbelief. His anger escalates as he clenches his fists.

"Listen, jackass, you best let me up or you will beg for your life once I get free!" yells Ian.

The man smiles and states, "Happy to see your threats are not only for children. Though, you must admit, I earn my hate through my actions upon you and children simply make mistakes."

Ian cannot believe he is being tormented by a psychopath that must talk with Nina's kids. Those brats had to have arranged this.

"Thank you for telling me who your working with on this. I will make sure each of those brats pay."

The man shakes his head and replies, "No, you misunderstand. I do not know the children. Simply saw various occasions of your torment and felt a need to retaliate. The breaking point for me to take action was upon hearing from a friend his daughter told him about how you tormented a young girl into thinking her exam with a gynecologist was so her mother could take a break from having sex with you. You gave her false information to make her fear the doctor as well as her mother's intentions."

Ian laughs and replies, "Dude, it was a joke. Her mother wants her on birth control to keep her from getting pregnant. The girl is not even having sex yet."

"True, but fear is not the answer. I plan to teach you just how the girl felt, but with a little more emphasis since you are a tough man whom feels kids should bow before your presence."

Ian watches the man step towards his head and reach for something behind him. He hears something on wheels moving towards him. As the man steps back to where he was, Ian sees him pulling a large metal tray on wheels. Ian begins to worry about the man's intentions as he views the medical instruments on the tray.

"Okay, I understand. Just let me go and we will talk about it."

The man quickly looks at him and simply shakes his head no.

"I will scream my head off. Your neighbors will hear me and call the cops. End this right now and no one needs to know."

"And yet you voice your opinion about crying with a slap to a child's head. You always state silence is golden. Have you changed your belief?"

Ian feels himself begin to shake as he states, "Ok, I admit I have been a bit harsh. Let me learn and save you in the process because I can scream very loud. Everybody will hear me and come after you for what you did. Just release me and we will work on it."

The man laughs and states, "Oh no, my neighbor's will never hear this. Sound insulation is a specialty of mine. So, go with the need to release the pain by yelling. After all, it will be the last words you ever say."

Chapter 21

JAVIER CRINGES AS HE enters the coroner's facility. He knows he does it each time he enters. Though he still attempts to figure out whether it is because he will face the beautiful hot-tempered Angela or if the building is simply too cold for his taste. Out of respect for her work on his case, he shall simply blame the temperature today. Life is just easier that way.

He walks to the receptionist to inquire about Angela, but sees her walk past him before he opens his mouth. He quickly diverts his movement as he states, "Angela, I need to have a few words with you. Is there somewhere we can talk?"

She stops and casts a quizzical expression as he steps to her. Not a hateful glare, but a "why the hell are you here" glare. He can work with such an expression.

Javier politely smiles and asks again, "Is there a room we can talk in? We found another body. However, I desire to discuss it a bit further with you because I am not sure if it is the same killer."

"How am I going to tell you if it is the same killer or not?" questions Angela.

To avoid conflict, he simply continues to smile and replies, "I am not going to be asking you to completely state whether it is the same killer. Can we please discuss this in private?"

She nods her head to the left and begins walking. He simply follows her rather than raise an argument on where they are going. She is looking beautiful once again. He would hate to see the look of anger she tends to use on him. Such a glare will definitely kill some beauty about her. Not much, but some. And not a lot, just a little.

She turns to the left and opens a door to what looks like a boardroom. She continues to hold the door and gestures for him to enter. Javier walks into the room and sits at the closest chair to the door. He feels as if he is being taken to the principal's office. He has to take control of this conversation before it gets brutal.

As Angela sits down, Javier states, "As you know, my chief requested assistance from the FBI since they have more resources and skill in dealing with serial killers. You and I both want to catch every piece of evidence to prosecute whoever is doing this. However, this recent murder may or may not be the same killer."

As Angela nods her head, she states, "You keep telling me that, but I am not sure how I have anything to offer other than the autopsies."

"Yes, I simply wanted to discuss this next victim with you because all the other victims had visible signs of their murder. Whether slices, brandings or photos, there was something stating this is murder! This last victim, we simply thought it was a guy who had a heart attack outside of the local elementary until we looked at his wrists and ankles."

Angela inhales deeply and asks, "Are all the school children terrified? Did any of them know the man? Obviously, I hope they do not, but it would ease you in identifying the man."

Javier watches as she stares at the table while shaking her head. Obviously, the death of the victim or the location which he was found affects her a bit. He hates when that happens.

"We cleared it all out prior to school starting. The night janitor is the one who came across the body. Thankfully, the principal was able to tell us who the man was because he apparently dates the mother of one of her students. I still need to talk with her, but wanted to talk with you first because if I am right, this guy is another victim and your going to find information while doing this autopsy."

Her eyes quickly divert to him and narrow upon him as she asks, "What kind of information?"

Javier knows she is probably hunting for information to argue, but he is not going to fall for it. Of course, he may be a bit too defensive considering their past arguments. Hell, he will give her the benefit of doubt and simply answer as if she thinks like everyone else.

"I am not exactly sure. However, all the victims had signs of what they did that apparently our killer does not like. Like the photos nailed to the body of the female who took over her father's pimping business. The killer apparently wanted us to find and release the captive prostitutes. My partner believes I am wrong and the guy simply had a heart attack while partaking in some very kinky sex. However, I do not agree with him."

Angela smiles and jokingly replies, "Well, I was not so informed about the photo victim until now. I do not read the newspaper. When I do an autopsy, I look at everything. So, if something is oddly inside this guy I am sure I shall find it and tell you how it got there. I just hope I do not vomit."

Javier laughs and replies, "I hope you are able to hold your stomach as well."

He would love to stay in this moment. She seems so relaxed and calm. Her beauty is definitely getting his blood to boil a bit. He begins tapping a finger on the table to calm himself down, which is something he generally cannot stand to hear or see. She definitely has an odd power over him.

"Is there anything else?" asks Angela.

Javier wishes he could think of something else to talk about, but since the conversation is about victims, he is extremely limited.

"No, I simply wanted to make you aware of what I believe so I can shove evidence in my partner's face. He believes it is simple medical issue during an adventure and not my psychopath."

Angela laughs as she rises from her chair. Nicholas quickly rises and moves to the door. He is a gentleman and it is time she found out a little about him. He opens the door and holds it as she steps out of the room.

"I will let you know as soon as the autopsy is available." states Angela.

"Thank you." replies Javier with a bright smile.

He closes the door as she walks away. He turns towards her and leans up against the door as he watches her. She is so beautiful and moves exquisitely. He wants more of their interactions to be more like this one. He truly believes she is an incredible person hiding behind something. He would love to free her from whatever it is. However, all that requires her permission and he doubts she is willing to give it. Well, maybe she will after getting to know him a little more. Though now, he must find out more about his victim. What did this piece of trash do to get killed and placed in front of an elementary school?

Chapter 22

AS THE BRIGHT SUN SHINES through the entryway windows, Nicholas looks around and descends the steps. He is still a bit tired, but knows there are more important things to do today than stay in bed.

One of the top things on his list is to contact the beautiful Angela and perhaps secure another date. Yet, it is still listed under some other tasks to do today. Though he doubts she will mind since one of the tasks above contacting her is to find out more about her brother. Now, he actually has his name, he can definitely make a more aggressive effort in finding the man.

As he enters the kitchen, Peter smiles wide and continues prepping what Nicholas assumes is lunch. He knows he did not oversleep lunch. At least, he thinks he did not. He has yet to look at a clock.

"Is that lunch, you are preparing?" asks Nicholas.

Without looking at him, Peter continues to work as he replies, "No, this duck is actually your supper. I am simply prepping it so the spices and herbs can work their way into its flavoring. Once completed, I shall begin your lunch, which shall be a wonderful cold soup accompanied with my wonderful bread."

Nicholas nods his head as he watches Peter. He has not had cold soup in a long time. With the sun shining so brightly, he imagines it shall be wonderful.

"I do not want to interfere with your work. So, perhaps while I am eating, we can discuss a few things?" asks Nicholas.

AMONGST DEATH 95

Peter shakes his head and replies, "As I told you many times, you do not interfere with my work when talking to me. I am a talented man who multitasks. Besides, I need to hear more about you and Angela. One date does not make a marriage."

Nicholas's eyes widen as he takes a seat on a stool. He has no clue why Peter is talking marriage after a simple date. True, it is not often he goes on dates. Especially, dates in which he asks someone out. Most of his dates in life were arranged through people he knew. He loves he took the initiative to ask Angela out, but a bit of closeness needs achieved before yanking out a ring. And, since Peter demanded he take her out, Nicholas is not sure he can take full credit for doing it.

"Stop with the marriage plotting when we have not even slept together. And do not start reciting it was God's way of telling me she was special. I did not sleep with her because I do not want a complicated relationship based on sex."

Peter rolls his eyes and states, "As if anyone can get close with you over a meal! I hate to tell you, but you already complicated your relationship with sex by kissing her. It may not have been a wham bam, but it is still of a sexual nature."

Nicholas buries his face in his hands and massages it a bit. He knew he should not have left a note telling Peter he kissed her goodnight. The note was not meant to brag. Simply an attempt to connect with Peter on a more personal level about how the date went. Perhaps? Okay, it may have been a bit of a brag...

Nicholas rests his hands on his lap and asks, "Do you still think you can find out information on her brother for me? I secured his name and know she is very interested in finding all she can on him."

As Peter takes the prepped duck and places it in the refrigerator, he replies, "I simply need a name. All of this happened in the past, which makes some people more willing to talk because the fear of talking diminishes a bit over time."

"Well, his name is Skip Summers. He had blond hair, but often liked to dye it. His eyes were green. Angela said he did not have problems talking with people with the exception of their father. She did not elaborate on that part though and I did not push for information."

Nicholas watches Peter wash his hands as he waits for a response. He is not sure the type of response he is expecting. What else is there to say than "I will look into it."

"If he had any kind of enjoyment of the sinful kind, then I am sure I shall find out something." states Peter.

Nicholas nods and feels a nap calling his name. He is sure the negative topic of conversation is causing him to desire sleep to dream better moments.

"On a different note, my lawyer left me a message stating the local police department is interested in the buildings I am opening for the kids and desires to meet me. I am not sure if I should agree."

Peter laughs as he pulls items out of the refrigerator to begin lunch. He begins sitting the items on the counter as he states, "Why someone, such as yourself, is concerned about meeting the police is beyond logic. You are a rich, white man building establishments to assist kids that simply need a bit of freedom to grow up. I doubt you will find harm with them."

Nicholas simply looks to the ground as Peter begins cutting vegetables. He understands Peter's view on the matter. However, there are so many more angles to the situation than just that. People always think so differently from one another, which means they may not desire to see the facilities open. Especially, when the kid is someone the police have had constant trouble with in their daily job. Nicholas knows he finds it near impossible to wish a positive future to someone he constantly sees doing wrong to others.

"Do you think they are looking for information?"

Nicholas watches Peter's face scrunch before he asks, "Information? If the police are looking to meet anyone, then they are looking to learn something. Whether it is about you or what you do is the better question to ask."

Nicholas feels his heart race. He hates confrontation and knows meeting them will probably lead to one. And, if it is Javier wishing to speak with him, then he is probably still attempting to steal Angela's heart, which Nicholas will not allow to happen. He takes a deep breathe to calm himself.

"Now, Nicholas, do not get yourself into a tizzy. They probably are interested in the facilities you are opening. After all, they will house kids the cops probably know and it is their job to keep them protected. With a serial killer on the loose, I am sure they want to make sure all is safe."

Nicholas smiles as he states, "Yes, but the serial killer is not looking to target the kids. The killer is targeting those that target them. I doubt the police really desire to find the killer."

Peter shakes his head and replies, "No, you are wrong there and I am happy to tell you why. Officers work to enforce the law. Laws are written to keep everyone living a safe day. Since people routinely target kids, the police are always looking to arrest them. If the serial killer kills all those targeting children, then there is no need for the laws and no need for the police. They search for the killer to ensure job safety."

Nicholas is in shock by his statement. Does Peter really believe the police only care about job security? Or does his statement mean one criminal does not trump another based on reason of the crime? Nicholas is sure the police have preferences of one crime over another. Unsure how to reply, he simply gazes in Peter's direction with his mouth slightly agape.

Before Nicholas can think of a reply, Peter laughs loudly and slaps the counter, "You are something else. I am just playing with you.

You and I both know crime will never end. The police will always be out there looking for someone."

Nicholas giggles and looks to the floor. He needs to work on his comprehension of humor. Hell, he needs to work on his comprehension of a lot of things. However, he is sure he needs to tighten the connection with Angela before Javier attempts to make a move.

Chapter 23

AS ANGELA STANDS AT the large wooden door and waits for Addie to answer it, she crosses her arms in attempt to feel some warmth. The air outside is not cold and the sun still shines. Yet, she feels as if her core lacks the proper temperature to live. She knows the cause is naught to do with her health. However, she does not fully understand why she is feeling this way either.

Addison opens the door as Angela attempts a welcoming smile.

"Oh dear, get in here. Your expression says a lot. Please have a seat in the living room as I prepare us some tea and you can tell me all about it." exclaims Addison.

Angela knows she should state a protest he is wrong in thinking something in her life went wrong. However, she is still unsure how to explain it. Nothing great nor absolutely bad happened to her. She simply needs internal warmth. Well, she thinks that is all she needs. Addie may develop a whole new thought of what she needs.

She walks into the living room and takes a seat on his large leather sofa. She knows she could look around at the photos on his walls and amuse herself until he joins her as she usually does, but she simply does not feel like doing so. The images are great and always changing because Addie feels one image does not dictate over another and diversity allows you to remember all the moments rather than a select few. She always argues he simply refuses to see the same images all the time. The argument never ends with them.

After a few silent minutes, Addison sits down beside her facing her with one leg bent on the sofa. He rests his elbow on the back of the couch and his head in his hand. He then simply looks at her. Angela knows he is waiting for her to talk.

"Addie, nothing really is wrong or right. I simply needed to connect after the autopsy I did today."

"What was so wrong with it? You do hundreds. Why is this one different? Are the serial murders starting to break you down?"

Angela changes her seating position to match Addie's, but does not rest her elbow on the back of the couch.

"In order for me to tell you anything, you have to promise me you will not use it for a news story."

Addie takes a deep breathe before replying, "Angela, murder is never my desired story. I enjoy the ones leading me to talking to people like Nicholas Payne. You know this and know I will not break your confidence."

Angela nods her head and states, "I did an autopsy today on the latest victim of the proclaimed "serial killer". Prior to doing it, Javier came to see me because he felt I may find evidence to prove to his partner the victim was killed by the serial murderer. Apparently, his partner does not believe the victim was killed by the same person."

"Did Javier state this to you as a demand or a request?"

Angela is taken aback at the odd question. She knows Javier and her do not have the best history with one another. Yet, she knows he is not the cause of what she is feeling right now. When she left the conversation with Javier, she actually felt they accomplished a truce with one another.

"Addie, Javier has nothing to do with this. I simply told you about him to introduce why this last autopsy was different. Javier was a gentleman when talking with him. We actually were very cordial to one another and simply discussed what he wanted me to prove."

Before Addie can reply, the kettle whistles in the kitchen.

Addie rises and states, "Hold on to that thought. I shall bring back the tea and some cookies."

Angela watches as he walks away. He disappears as she begins to wonder if the conversation with Javier simply triggered her mind into reading more into the autopsy than needed. Perhaps knowing she may find the evidence defining the same killer when the police did not know took her mentally connecting with the victim a bit more than ever desired. Not that she would ever connect with the victim if he were alive. What she found in the autopsy proved the type of man he was and probably defined why the killer killed him. After all, the killer seems to have an anger towards each victim and is proud to give away the secrets. Yet, this one was slightly different.

Addison hands her a cup of tea and places a tray of cookies on the living room table. Angela blows a bit over the cup and takes a sip.

"Angela, I shall never understand your ability to drink hot tea without any sugar." states Addison as he sits down.

Angela grins and states, "My parents never allowed us the option. My father always stated, "If a drink is made suitable, then it does not require decoration." My brother, Skip, hated the statement because he felt Def Leppard attempted to tell the world sugar and love require each other to exist, but our father was denying us the ability to see it. Rather than argue, I simply never drank tea with sugar."

"Sounds to me like Skip was arguing a sex life rather than sugar in tea."

Angela bursts into laughter. She does not know if Skip was arguing such, but it is possible.

"Okay, back to the issue. What is so traumatic about this autopsy? You do them all the time. Why is this one different?" inquires Addison.

"A lot of it was what I found when doing the autopsy. The body without my incisions appeared fine with the exception of marks on wrists and ankles. It was not until I was inside the body that I was able to see what the killer did and what he used."

"Was it done before or after the victim died?"

Angela places her tea on the living room table as she states, "Before he died for some and after for others. I submitted blood work for a toxicology report because he died from something in his system rather than the things I found."

"Found?"

Angela nods her head and replies, "Yes, he had items inserted through his rectum and down his throat. Though the ones found in his throat were done after the victim died."

"What were these things? Obviously, Javier will use the items as evidence, but what is their intentional meaning?"

Angela pulls her legs up on the couch as she turns towards Addison. She knows she should not tell him the details because it really is unethical. However, the autopsy she did today was too vulgar to endure herself.

"The rectum contained items wrapped in plastic. I asked the forensic crew if it was safe to unwrap them. They basically sprinted over to where I was with their equipment in tow. At the end of it all, they found a plastic toy kitten, a picture of four kids, a piece of paper with writing, a ball and some of those reusable ice cubes, which were frozen when inserted."

"What did the paper say?" asks Addison.

Angela shrugs and states, "I do not know. I did not read it. The forensic crew did not like what the letter stated though. One even told me, "I am glad the bastards dead.", which may have been what triggered this depression."

"Probably so." replies Addison.

Angela sees the stress she is causing him because of the look on his face. He appears as if he walked into a funeral. Definitely not the look he had when answering the door.

"Not to bring you to an even more negative level, but the items in his throat were different. There was a bracelet, a baseball with bat key chain, a pacifier and a plastic toy bike."

Addison looks to the floor and states, "Obviously this victim pissed someone off about some kids. Where did they find the body?"

"At one of the local elementary schools. The forensics crew sent a photo of the picture to Javier so he could possibly track down the children in it."

Angela continues to watch Addison as he takes a sip of tea. She realizes her body does feel lighter than when she arrived. The knowledge of all that must have been the overbearing stress she arrived with.

"Is there anything happy we can talk about?" asks Angela.

Addison takes a sip of tea and states, "Yes, I bought a wonderful afghan today."

Angela cannot hold back her laughter. Only Addie is able to transition a dark serious discussion into a conversation about nothing more than him, which is exactly why she is here. She simply wishes Nicholas was in the mix as well, but she is willing to wait for it to happen.

Chapter 24

JAVIER SITS AT HIS desk looking at the new evidence the forensic team gave him. He does not have the autopsy report yet and is dying to read it. However, all these items definitely prove he was right about it being the same killer. Yet, none of it is making him happy. This killer is killing the people Javier does not like, but the way it is done is a bit psychotic. How long until the killer makes a mistake and kills an innocent person? Or, simply runs out of sick guilty people and moves on to simple crimes, such as parking tickets?

Javier examines a picture of children as Steve sits in the chair next to his desk. Javier looks to him and states, "Next time we do not agree, I am going to place money on it. I was right. The same killer killed the elementary school victim."

Steve rolls his eyes and replies, "You won one argument. I take it this stuff is the new evidence."

"Yes, but we do not have the autopsy report yet and I am told a toxicology report will be on the way as well. In the meantime, we need to find out who the kids in this picture are and if they know anything about this writing." replies Javier as he holds up the photo and piece of paper that came as evidence.

Steve reads the large black writing on the piece of paper. His fists clench as he finishes reading it. Javier understands his anger. He wants to bring the guy back to life so he can have a few rounds with the guy. Not to necessarily kill him again, but a beating seems justified.

"Well, it does definitely show our killer is out for vengeance. Each case he tends to leave a reasoning. Do you think he knows the kids? Or, is it possible he saw our victim doing something the killer did not like?"

Javier places the evidence on his desk and leans back into his chair. The killer obviously does not like his victims, but knowing how close he is with each victim is a bit mind boggling. The killer has to be in contact with the victims in order to know the things that are being given as reason for killing them. Looking upon a certain lifestyle will lead them to nothing though. The victims are of various race, various financial worth and live in various neighborhoods around the city. None of the victims seem to link to one another with the exception the same person killed them all.

"The killer knows of the victims' flaws. There has to be some type of connection with each victim. I was leaning towards it all being sex crime related, but this picture and paper leans more towards an abusive father, step-father or mother's boyfriend. Did you learn anything at the school? We now have a larger image of the picture I forwarded to you if the school staff had trouble viewing the digital one on your phone."

Steve smiles wide and states, "I not only learned who the children are, but also the observed mentality of the mother, which is workable but not always understanding benefit for children she birthed. Apparently, she analyzes things a bit better without her boyfriend around according to the school secretary. I know you want to speak with her as much as I do. So, I avoided running to her home and beginning an interrogation. Though from what I heard and seeing all of this, I doubt she will want to talk to us because she does have a loyalty to the victim, which means she may not desire to speak of his flaws."

Javier shakes his head and replies, "I believe we will have better luck with the children. With these items, they obviously are thought of being victims by the killer. It is possible the killer is connected in some way to the kids rather than the mother's boyfriend. Or, possibly the kids' father, if he is in the picture, but I doubt it because if my kids had to deal with this crap, the boyfriend and mother would have died an accidental death a long time ago."

"Do you think any of it is sexual?"

Javier looks to Steve and knows his next comment will either be a stress relief or a stab in the heart. The thought of looking for justice for a victim that sexually tormented a child rips his heart out. The logic of having to hunt down the person that committed the crime you are happy they committed is hard to keep a grasp on.

"I think this one was more about simple abuse and power over the abuser. Apparently, the abuser rejoiced in power over the kids. We need to find out more about this guy before we can really rule anything though. For all we know, the killer may have disliked one thing and not realized another flaw of the victim."

Steve nods as he replies, "Yeah, and all of the things the killer did not like are different from one another. Our killer apparently gets around and learns about people. The killer either works a job that takes them throughout town or socializes in a lot of locations with a lot of people."

Javier looks around the office as he thinks about what Steve stated. He agrees with it a bit. However, if it is a job taking the killer around, he doubts the work is anything manual labor. This killer knows how to kill people and make it look like much was not done to the victim. So, the killer is educated in some way.

"Hey, did you hear back about meeting with Nicholas Payne?" asks Steve.

Javier shakes his head and replies, "No, his lawyer said he was able to tell him about the request, but they have been unable to alter schedules."

"I guess he simply wants to get back with you on it rather than give you five minutes of introduction to keep kids safe. Prick!"

Javier is not sure why Steve takes offense to the lawyer's reply. He can imagine Nicholas Payne is busy since he does work with...

Javier feels as if a bolt of lightning struck him from above. He looks to Steve and asks, "Do you think it is possible our killer is connected to Nicholas Payne? The man is opening two facilities to assist emancipated kids, which are vulnerable to the people our killer is killing. He has not been in town long from what I hear and the killings just recently began."

Steve laughs and asks, "Do you honestly believe our killer is the wealthy Nicholas Payne?"

Javier shakes his head and states, "No, not exactly. Of course, it could be him. I simply wonder if someone he connected with in order to bring change is taking the whole thing a little too far."

He watches Steve's eyes briefly expand as he thinks about it. Javier knows it is possibly connected to Mr. Payne, but he is not giving the man clearance either. He could just as easily be the killer.

"Well, you have a valid point. Guess we need to stress the meeting with the lawyer a bit more." states Steve.

"I shall do that. Meanwhile, try to set up a meeting with the mother and ask her if it is okay to talk with the children. If she denies us access to them, we will simply get children services involved. With our evidence, she will have a hard time pushing them away from the kids."

Steve rises as he chuckles and states, "I shall do as told. And since I can be such a nice gentleman, I am sure the mother will arrange for us to speak with the kids."

Javier shakes his head and replies, "When you wake up from that dream, I will tell you what I was able to arrange to talk with Nicholas Payne. Even if they cannot meet with us soon, the lawyer may be able to tell me about the people who work with them to make these places happen."

Javier watches Steve nod and walk away. He then begins looking around his desk for the lawyer's business card. He doubts a meeting will take place anytime soon, but the lawyer does have information that is possibly useful and Javier is going to demand it. May take some harassment during conversation, but damn it, the man is going to give them something.

Chapter 25

ANGELA OPENS HER APARTMENT door and throws her purse on the hallway credenza. Her whole thought of this evening involves relaxing, eating a good meal and possibly watching a great movie. Whether she does it all alone, she does not care. She simply wants a calmness in her night.

As she enters her living room and kicks off her heels, she notices her home phone has voicemail. She imagines it is a telemarketer of some sort or Addie with a grand new plan of some sort. She walks over and hits the button.

> *"Message 1: Hello, Angela. I was wondering if you would like to have dinner with me tonight at my place. My chef is making a wonderful steak dinner I believe you would enjoy. Afterwards, maybe, I could give you a tour of my home. Or, something else...if you prefer. No need to call back. You can simply head on over at your convenience. Hope to see you.*
>
> *End of Messages"*

Angela feels her heart skip a beat as she begins to quickly undress and run to her closet. With the idea of relaxation in her mind, she never thought to expect a call from the wonderful Nicholas Payne. And he thinks a tour of his home may be proper? Hell, only if it ends in the bedroom. As Angela looks through her wardrobe, she intends to select the outfit that will make him think there is no better place to end the tour.

As Angela takes a sip of wine, she watches Nicholas take his final bite of dessert. She finished hers a minute ago and patiently waits for him. With the sex appeal he has tonight, she does not mind waiting at all.

His unruly dark hair accents his face properly as he chews while looking at his plate. His jaw muscles appear a bit with each bite. Angela is not sure why, but it is turning her on even more. Perhaps it is the visualization of the animal within him.

"Well, I am definitely taking too much time and making you wait. Since we are both finished, would you like a tour of my home? It is rather large, but very well crafted." states Nicholas.

Angela sits her wine glass down and smiles widely as she replies, "Of course, Nicholas. Shall we take the plates to the kitchen?"

"Oh no need to do so. At some point, Peter shall take care of it." states Nicholas as he rises from his chair and walks towards Angela.

Thankfully, the table is a bit long for just the two of them dining. She is able to rise and stand a bit sensually as he looks at her with each step. She prays he is eating the view up and with the wicked smile beginning to cross his face, he may be doing just that.

Upon reaching her location, he walks behind her and pushes in her chair. Angela feels a chill down her spine as he touches her back and states, "You look wonderful tonight."

His hand slides down her back and rests around her waist as they begin walking out of the dining room. Angela attempts to keep her hands from shaking with each step. She so desires to simply turn to him and begin kissing, but knows it will ruin the moment a bit and only lead to simply fucking rather than a very romantic, sexual encounter, which is her preference. She takes a deep breathe in attempt to calm herself.

"I believe you have seen most of the down stairs when you were here for the dinner party and for lunch with Winston. If we go up the stairs here, I can show you the library and the atrium."

"You have an atrium on the second floor? Is that not an odd location?" asks Angela.

Nicholas chuckles and replies, "I thought so as well. However, from what I heard from other people, I understood it a bit more. When the original owner had the place built, his mother lived with him and his wife as well as their children. Apparently, the mother despised his wife and the wife felt the same. In order to keep peace within the home, he built a music room downstairs so his wife whom loved music could teach the children and an atrium on the second floor so his mother whom loved plants could pass her time away from his wife. As the children aged, he also built a greenhouse off of the kitchen to keep the children busy. I was told it worked out very well for him."

Angela laughs and asks, "What did he do while everyone was occupied? Or, did he simply spend his free time visiting each room?"

As they begin ascending the staircase, Nicholas replies, "I am not too sure. However, I am confident his day involved a few drinks. So perhaps the library or his personal study was his room of retreat."

Reaching the top of the stairs, Nicholas motions for them to walk to the left towards a hallway. Angela is amazed how large this home is and wonders how only one person can live in it. Yet, she feels a bit stupid for thinking so because he really is not alone. Between the dinner party and his personal chef, there are people here at various times, including herself.

As they turn to walk down a hallway, Nicholas states, "Do not hold the condition of the atrium against me. The previous owner hated plants and let them all die. I have been working on restoring it, but a lot of the plants need to grow more in order to look like a true atrium."

Angela looks to him and replies, "All things need a little love to grow."

As Nicholas chuckles, Angela notices a door as they walk past it. The door is shut and has an ornate metal sign stating "Dark Room". She looks straight ahead as she wonders how many people even use dark rooms now. She imagines someone of this wealth in the past was fascinated with photographs and the ability to develop them at home, but she believes Nicholas does not think too much of it because he did not mention it existing.

"And here we are." states Nicholas as he opens a door and holds it in place for her to enter.

Angela enters and looks around the room as she feels Nicholas approaching her from behind. He stops when he is about an inch away and she can feel her hormones kicking in. His hands rest on her hips as he states, "As I said earlier, it is all a work in progress. The roses still need to develop, but the tulips are doing very well. Peter did me a favor and planted them before I arrived."

Angela does another scan of the room and then turns around as his hands remain stationed on her hips. She looks into his eyes and smiles as her hands rise to rest upon his shoulders.

"Your work in progress shall be a beautiful show piece one day." states Angela.

A lustful gaze crosses his face as he states, "Only in attempt to catch up with your beauty."

Before she can think of a reply, his lips are on hers and he pulls her closer. She wraps her arms around his neck as his hands slide to her buttocks. She feels the heat within her grow as he opens her mouth with his tongue.

Wanting to see his wonderful body, she begins to unbutton his shirt. His hands quickly slide over hers as he breaks from the kissing and states, "Wait, if this is going to continue the way I want, we should find a better room."

Happy he desires the same outcome as she, Angela replies, "Lead the way."

The wicked grin she knows once again appears as he abruptly sweeps her off her feet and begins carrying her out of the atrium. The combination of shock and lust has her desiring him even more. She begins kissing and sucking on his neck as takes her somewhere.

As she begins sucking on his earlobe, she hears him open a door. She begins to move her arm within his shirt to feel those wonderful muscles. She returns to kissing his neck as she feels him letting go of her legs.

Once standing, he claims her mouth and begins unzipping the back of her dress. She manages to unfasten the last button on his shirt and yanks it off. To the floor it falls as she quickly kicks off her shoes. His mouth claims hers once again as he begins walking her towards something that she is hoping is his bed. With each step backwards, she works on releasing his belt. She feels her brassiere disappear and his hand clamp over her breast. She is in flames as she manages to undo his trousers.

She feels a bed against the back of her legs. She lowers herself on it while sliding back as he follows her movement. She gasps and clings to his neck as he uses his tongue to play with her nipple. He begins to suck as he pulls off her panties.

With her panties gone, his hands return to her breasts as he runs his tongue down her belly to her clitorises. His fingers play with her nipples as his tongue begins to work magic. Angela clenches the bed covering as her pleasure begins to build more and more. His hands disappear from her breasts while his tongue continues to find the appropriate spot.

He suddenly replaces his tongue's position with a few fingers and licks his way back to her mouth. Engaged in an intense kiss, she can feel his manhood against her.

"Do you have a condom?" asks Angela as he continues the massages and begins kissing her neck.

Rather than answer, he simply reaches over to a nightstand drawer and picks one out. Angela takes it from his hand and states, "I will put it on."

As she rips open the packaging, he continues to kiss her as his fingers enter her. She gasps as his fingers work magically.

She quickly takes out the condom and places it on him. She returns to exploring his body with her hands. Within seconds, he is in between her legs and begins entering her. He feels her breast with each thrust as she continues to kiss his neck.

Wanting to feel him even more, she wraps her legs around his waist as she kisses him. The thrusts grow stronger and more tantalizing with each moment. Angela feels her climax progressing as his thrusts progress. Moans begin to escape her lips as she claws at his back. With each thrust, she feels her body respond even more.

His moans begin to match hers. She feels her climax take place as he reaches his release. She breathes heavily as he roles onto his back and attempts to catch his breath.

As both attempt to regain normal breathing, Angela roams the room with her eyes and asks, "Is this your bedroom?"

Nicholas chuckles and replies, "Yes."

Angela feels her breathing begin to calm and simply relaxes. Now she knows where she is within the home nothing really else really matters to her. She is sure they will find continuation of what just happened.

Chapter 26

JAVIER AND STEVE STAND quietly outside courtroom doors. Javier managed to get lucky during a brief conversation when a patrol officer mentioned attorney Fred Durham was at the courthouse to present a case. Javier does not know which case nor does he care. He simply wants a little talking time with the elusive Mr. Durham. Nicholas Payne would be a bit better to speak with, but Fred is a start.

The court doors open and a few people begin to file out. Javier walks closer to the doors in attempt to view Fred. He sees him loading his legal attache with documents he brought to court. Rather than approach the man, Javier decides to wait for him to exit the courtroom. This way Fred does not feel threatened nor a need to defend in the conversation. If he allows him to have a sense of power and authority, then Fred is more likely to answer questions.

"He is walking are way. Shouldn't we approach him?" asks Steve.

Javier quickly shakes his head and looks at the ground. As soon as Fred exits the courtroom, he shows his badge and states, "Pardon me, Mr. Durham. I am Javier Alexander. This is my partner Steve Olsen. I spoke to your secretary several times in attempt to reach you. I simply need some information."

He watches Fred relax his stance before he asks, "What kind of information are you looking to obtain? I cannot talk with you about the upcoming operation of my client's facilities."

Javier desires to laugh at the fact Durham talks about the appropriate client instantly without Javier mentioning a name. He will assume the secretary informed him of the conversations.

Javier smiles and replies, "We are not looking for that type of information. The operation of your facility is your concern. With a serial killer on the loose, we simply are looking at all possible directions of identifying the killer. We are seeing items of evidence that cause us to believe the killer may either have a connection to the facility or is influenced by it."

Fred's eyes narrow as he states, "I can assure you Mr. Payne has nothing to do with these murders. He is simply a wealthy man whom occupies his time with good causes."

Javier shakes his head and states, "We in no way think he has anything to do with the murders. However, there is possibility someone has viewed Mr. Payne's causes and found influence. All the murders seem to have a reasoning as if the killer is attempting to protect society. We worry about the killer working their way into Mr. Payne's causes. And a bigger concern is finding out if they are already within his operations or simply using him for inspiration. Whoever our killer is, they seem infatuated with correcting society's problems, which is somewhat like your client."

Fred motions them towards the benches in the hallway. After all of them take a seat, he states, "I worry a lot for Mr. Payne. His wealth does tend to draw a lot of people. And, he does not associate with the best people to know. His personal chef is an ex-convict. And he recently began to become a bit infatuated with a woman whom I do not know. I offered to run a check on her, but he absolutely refused."

"Do you normally run checks on those around him?" asks Steve.

"No, I cannot say I do because he normally does not date, which is why I am concerned about him with her. Though I do normally run company checks on those we do business with prior to entering into contract."

Javier shrugs and states, "Smart move when doing business. You want to make sure they are capable and trustworthy of actually fulfilling the contract. What is this woman's name? Do you know where she works?"

"Her name is Angela Summers. And, I only know the name from talking with his chef. Personal information generally is not exchanged in our relationship. I try to learn more about Nicholas's personal life, but he does not really like to talk about it."

Javier hears Steve cough and desires to smack him. He turns his head to look at him and Steve states, "I am going to get a cup of coffee."

Javier watches him rise and race away. He hopes the coward chokes on his coffee. How is it the mysterious Nicholas Payne managed to secure Angela Summers? Better yet, why did he not realize he has already seen them together? Instead of playing this tag game with Nicholas Payne's lawyer, he could have simply asked his girlfriend to hook them up.

"Mr. Durham, I apologize for my partner's issue. Though I can give you a bit of information on Angela Summers. She works for the Coroner's Office and ironically performs the autopsies on the murder victim's."

Javier watches Mr. Durham begin to look quizzical. He knows he needs to change the direction of the conversation before Mr. Durham concentrates on finding more about Angela in attempt to protect his "prized" client.

"Now, you state he hired an ex-convict for his personal chef. Obviously, the man is capable of performing the work. Otherwise, I am sure he would lose employment. Did you run a background check on him? Is he linked to other criminals?"

He leans close to Javier and states, "Between you and me, I can tell you I did run a check on the man. The man did apparently learn his lesson and changed his life around. However, I cannot guarantee he is not around other criminals. He does mentoring work with troubled teens as well as ex-convicts attempting to throw away the past."

As Mr. Durham returns to his original seating position, Javier wonders if the chef is the possible link. Not necessarily the killer, but someone the killer sees or hears.

"Is it possible for you to arrange a meeting with Mr. Payne at his home? I may get the opportunity to speak with the chef as well and possibly find a lead."

He watches Mr. Durham tense a bit. He knows the man probably pushes his connections with Mr. Payne by suggesting such things.

"I will arrange something and have my secretary tell you when."

"Thank you, Mr. Durham." states Javier as he extends his hand.

They shake hands and rise from their seats. As Mr. Durham walks away, Javier wonders if he should talk with Angela about keeping her mouth shut. Obviously, she has not done anything inappropriate, but if she talks about her work in any way, the killer may hear about it and begin to cover tracks a bit better.

Chapter 27

THE DAY IN THE OFFICE is a bit calmer than usual. Angela is not required to autopsy another victim. Her sexual desire is calm thanks to a wonderful Nicholas Payne. She has not heard from him since her departure from his home the morning after. However, since the departure was nice and only a day ago, she is not really annoyed with it. And, her lunch today is rather appealing, which is odd for their cafeteria.

As she takes a sip of her drink, Winston drops her wrapped sandwich on the table and abruptly takes a seat. Wide-eyed, Angela wonders what causes her to be in such a mood. She rarely sees Winston act in such an aggressive, throw all to the wind manner.

"Troubles, Winston?"

Winston rolls her eyes and replies, "Yes and no. If I tell you my annoyance with one thing, will you tell me about another event?"

Angela is a bit curious on what is troubling her, but she has no clue what she desires to hear about. She is a friend and they talk about a lot of things. Yet, Angela does not desire for her to know everything about her life. She likes to decide on her personal privacy, not gamble it.

Winston takes a bite of her sandwich as Angela states, "I am not sure I can tell you anything since I do not know what you want to hear from me. Why make a demand to tell me what is annoying you?"

Winston swallows her bite and states, "It is not a demand. Simply a request for information on your recent dinner with Nicholas Payne you failed to tell me about. I figured I could tell you about my annoyance with the FBI agents harassing me this morning and you could lift up my spirits by telling me information they desired."

Angela is a bit thrown back by her statement. She did not tell Winston about her night with Nicholas because she did not tell anyone. She wanted to keep it personal. Besides, she would be stupid to brag to everybody about it. She does not yet know if his goal was only the one night.

"Why were FBI agents speaking with you? And, how did you find out about Nicholas? I have not told anyone because I have not heard from him yet."

Winston's shoulders sink as she replies, "I do not know even which night it took place. Has it been a long time?"

If Winston did not look so depressed about her not hearing from him yet, Angela would tell her the conversation is over. Though, why are the FBI talking with her? Better yet, does the FBI know about their night together? Is Big Brother breathing over her shoulder without her knowing?

"I stayed with him the night before yesterday. How does the FBI know such a thing? And, why are they asking about Nicholas?"

Winston nearly chokes on her drink before replying, "Angela, I am sorry and did not mean to cause a panic about the FBI. They simply asked me some questions about what I knew of your and Nicholas's relationship. They are here to track down the serial killer. After speaking with Javier a bit, he expressed concern the killer may kill to show support of Nicholas's organizations. Javier stated he just recently realized he is the same Nicholas you date. Since I was with you at the mall incident, the FBI asked me about your relationship."

Angela is not sure to get excited or cry. People are already speaking about them having a relationship, which sounds great to her. Yet, she is not sure she can call it a relationship.

"I am not sure we have one yet. However, I doubt Javier is aware of such since we do not really talk about the incident at the mall. However, you have yet to tell me how you knew I stayed the night with Nicholas."

With a grimace, Winston states, "I doubt they know anything like that. After the FBI and I talked, I called Peter to make sure I was not harassing you with some bullshit the FBI thought they knew. He told me you recently had dinner and afterwards entertainment, but was not sure on relationship status. Did you sleep with Nicholas? How was it?"

Angela shakes her head in disbelief. One incident at a mall is causing the whole town to gossip about a relationship that may not even exist. If she had spoken with Javier about what happened, she doubts her and Nicholas's names would be connected by the FBI.

"Yes, we slept together and I enjoyed it very much." states Angela as she begins to blush.

Winston mouths "Wow" and takes another bite of her sandwich. Angela looks to her lunch and desires to vomit on the whole plate. She is not concerned with Winston knowing about the evening, but how many other people know? If Peter insinuates a possible intimate connection to Winston, then how many other people speak with him about the same thing? Though if Peter is willing to talk about it, then Nicholas may desire a better connection to her than she thought. Right? Peter would not threaten his employment status with false stories. Or, would he?

"Winston, until I hear back from Nicholas, I really prefer not to talk about it."

Chapter 28

THE EVENING BEGINS with Wilson Smith wondering into the local liquor store. Quickly moving through the aisles he is familiar with, he grabs his nightly poison and takes it to the counter.

"Sure about this, Wilson? Your kid may need money for lunch tomorrow." states the sales clerk.

Wilson simply throws the money down on the counter and walks out. He knows he is walking away from a few pennies he is owed back, but getting a sip of this bottle is more important to him right now. He quickly twists off the cap and takes a few gulps. The heavenly liquid travels down to his stomach and he feels more like a human being. Those morning withdraws are beginning to get harsher each day. Of course, if Gabrielle would lay off on him about "responsibilities", then he probably would not need this liquid courage.

After securing the cap back on, Wilson begins walking down the street. He is not sure of his exact destination, but knows it definitely is not home. Not too many friends care to drink anymore due to jobs, kids, spouses or medical issues. So, a friend's place really is not an option.

On the corner of the block, he takes a left towards the city park. He knows no one is supposed to be there after hours. However, those kids' play areas do offer a covering where he can relax, drink and savor the time. God knows he spent many a time there with kids in not so enjoyable moments.

Reaching the park, he heads towards the slides. With all those tunnels, he is sure he can find a comfortable spot. He is not the size he use to be, but believes he can still fit.

He begins to ascend the stairs while he looks around to make sure no one is watching. The last thing he needs is someone believing his moment to cherish a drink is a sign he is actually a pedophile and getting his rocks off on the playground.

He reaches the tunnel and decides against entering one. Standing at the entrance makes him realize his size and its interior a bit more. They look larger from the outside. Or, perhaps, his kid is simply small. Does not really matter to him though. He simply decides to sit on the platform. He looks over his bottle and takes the cap off. With a long, slow drink, he is enticed to lean back and relax.

As he continues to drink, he allows his eyes to wander around the park. He is not expecting to see anything, but keeping an eye out is proper. You never know when someone will come along and attempt something they should not attempt. And, with a serial killer running around in the city, safety should be everyone's concern. Though from what he hears, the serial killer is killing those that are sex addicts. He is not too sure why a sex addict is a horrible thing, but apparently the killer does not like them.

He takes another drink and looks to the left near the wooded area of the park. He has never walked on the trails of the wooded area even though his kid asked him many times. He is sure it is the best place in the park to sit and drink right now, but definitely not the safest. All kinds of crazy things could happen back there.

As if his thoughts were predicting movement, Wilson's body stiffens as he watches someone drag a person off of the trail. It is too dark and far away for Wilson to see any facial details, but a man in black clothing seems to control the body he is dragging. Perhaps, the other guy overdosed or passed out from excessive drinking. He does not appear to be moving in any way.

Wilson takes another drink as he watches the man in black re-enter the trail area. He quickly caps his drink and continues to watch. Why would the man go back in the woods when his buddy obviously needs some kind of assistance? Whether its a bed or an EMT, Wilson does not understand why he went back into the woods. Unless...the man in black is hooking up with the guy's girlfriend in the woods and simply brought him out of the woods so they did not awaken him. Yes, that is the scoundrel's ticket.

After a chuckle, he unscrews the cap and takes another swig. He shakes his head and laughs at the antics that must be going on in the woods. He remembers those days of being a younger guy. Everything was about the fun times. Unlike now, now everything is about blame and responsibilities.

As he takes another drink, Wilson sees the man in black walk out of the woods once again, except this time he is carrying something. It is not a girlfriend nor another man. He appears to carry a dead dog. At least, he assumes it is dead for it is not making any movement and the limbs seem to bounce with each step the man takes.

Wilson caps his drink once again and watches closely as the man in black positions his friend after pulling his pants down. He then lays the dog down in front of him. Wondering if he should call the cops or simply say something to the man in black, Wilson sets his bottle aside.

The man in black takes something out of his pocket and shoves it into the other man's mouth. Wilson begins to look around to see if anyone else is witnessing this. He is not sure what exactly he is viewing, but it is not normal.

"Have a wonderful death you sick bastard!" yells the man in black before he runs back into the woods.

Wilson wants to chase after the man to get an answer about all of this, but he is not sure he could bring him down. The man has a sturdy build. A build much better than Wilson's. He continues to look around for someone to assist him. Yet, there is no one. He knows he has to find someone.

He grabs up his bottle and quickly climbs down from the play area. He is not familiar with anyone living around here, but the liquor store is still open. Taking off in a sprint, Wilson prays the sales clerk will believe him.

Chapter 29

CLOUDS COVER THE SUN as a slight breeze crosses Nicholas's backyard. He looks out the atrium windows to see how the weather is unfolding. Peter told him the weather outside was enjoyable today without the harsh sun rays. Yet, he does not desire to be out there and is not sure why. He simply wishes all to disappear for a bit so he can figure some life details out.

Developing a bit of a thirst, he leaves the atrium and heads to the kitchen. He has no intention of striking up conversation with Peter as he prepares lunch. Yet, he knows it will probably happen. Though, today, he will let Peter take the rare role of instigating and leading the conversation. He shall feel accomplished with such an honor. Almost a Christmas in July gift, except it is not July nor the twenty-fifth.

He enters the kitchen and is welcomed by a warm smile from Peter. He simply nods and heads to the refrigerator. He is not sure what will quench his thirst, but there must be something worthwhile in the refrigerator.

As the bright blue light shines, Nicholas looks at each shelf. Full of various sodas, juices and waters on multiple shelves. Yet, nothing particular stands out as refreshing. He simply grabs a bottle of water and shuts the door. He begins twisting off the cap as he turns around.

"Are you battling anything particular today? Or, simply attempting to avoid conversation?" questions Peter.

Nicholas wonders if his mood is so obvious or Peter simply knows how to analyze his actions. Either case is not something he wishes Peter to strive in mastering.

"Are you insinuating I should tell you something before your curiosity causes your brain to burst?" states Nicholas in a very dry tone.

"Oh, vicious boy today. And here I thought your time with the beautiful Angela may have tamed you for a bit." replies Peter with a look of amazement.

Nicholas looks to the floor and chuckles. Damn, he must be in a foul mood to forget about Angela. He has not spoken with her for two days, which was the morning after they had sex. He needs to connect with her again. Perhaps, it is the cause of this unusual mood.

"Tell me, Peter. After you have been intimate with a woman, how long before you contact them again and how do you do it? I imagine you do not simply pick up the phone and invite them over again. The term "booty call" is never a positive term from what I hear."

Peter places Nicholas's lunch in front of him as he asks, "Are you telling me you never had sex with a woman more than once?"

Nicholas blushes and replies, "No, I am attempting to make a valid effort in knowing her a bit more without offending her."

As Nicholas begins eating, Peter chuckles and begins cleaning up after himself. Nicholas continues to eat and waits for a reply. He knows Peter will eventually think of an answer.

"Since you apparently desire a relationship with the beautiful Angela, you must send the lady a beautiful arrangement of flowers along with a card. And not a regular flower card! Something with a meaning that is enhanced with a hand written message from you."

Nicholas grimaces and states, "I am not too sure about doing it. I already sent her a flower to ask her out. The flower simply had the flower card the florist supplies though. So, there is still room for improvement, I guess."

"What do you know about her personal enjoyments? Anything?" questions Peter.

Nicholas looks at his fork and thinks on the question. He knows a few of her enjoyments from conversation. Though the biggest enjoyment he could supply is finding her brother.

"Have you found any information on her brother?"

Peter gives a stern look and states, "No and do not change the subject."

Nicholas's eyes widen as he replies, "I am not changing the subject. You asked what she enjoys and I know her brother is at the top of the list."

Peter rolls his eyes and asks, "Do you enjoy her thinking about her brother more than you?"

Nicholas takes the question as rhetorical and simply begins to eat again. If Peter is not going to simply offer a few suggestions without interrogation, then he will ask someone else. Perhaps, Addison is available.

"Nicholas, you can sulk all you like. Yet, sulking is not going to assist you in not looking like an ignorant ass in front of Angela because you are too cowardly to simply call her and talk after having sex. Oh, wait, has the unusual pleasure fried your mind?"

Nicholas throws his fork onto his plate and glares at Peter. He knows the last comment is simply to get him to begin conversation. However, it is still very insulting and his ego jumped to the brink of anger.

"No, Peter, my climax did not fry my brain. I simply was tied up in things the past couple of days. Then, realizing I forgot to call her, I slumped into a bit of a panic mode. She is probably insulted and simply wants to yell at me. What if I call, she yells and hangs up on me? Is it not better to entice her to be nice with the first moment of conversation?"

Nicholas watches Peter's face clear of all emotion. As Peter simply stares at him, he feels a bit insecure.

"Nicholas, I now understand you have no knowledge about a woman and how she thinks. First of all, a woman is always happy when you call her after you have had sex. Some begin bitching to friends if you did not call back in their ideal time frame, but it vanishes upon calling them. As for "enticing" a woman, you need to understand they are not dogs. Yes, some money grubbers do simply want you to buy them things as if they need toys. However, I doubt the beautiful Angela is such a woman."

Nicholas wonders if he should listen to him a bit more. He knows Peter is more relationship orientated than himself and is more than likely correct. So why does he feel the way he does? Well throwing ego to the side, he is slightly afraid of what Angela may become in his life and he is not sure how he shall take it if for some crazy reason she begins to reject him.

Not desiring Peter to learn more of his flaws, Nicholas begins to eat again as he thinks on what to say when he calls Angela. He may not know too much about women, but he is pretty sure saying "Hey, come over and have sex with me." is not the appropriate beginning of a conversation. Well, in some cases, it may be the perfect beginning of a conversation. However, he doubts Angela would enjoy it. He will just think of what to talk about and wing the conversation. Any other way seems a bit monsterous.

Chapter 30

ANGELA TOSSES HER USED examine clothes into the laundry bin and exits the preparation room. She officially is done for the day and simply desires to go home for a nice glass of wine. Perhaps listen to some Bach play as she thinks about calling Nicholas. He still has not called her nor made any indication of enjoying their time together.

She is not angry at him. She simply wishes to know if all with him is now at an end or if he is simply busy. However, she is not even sure if she can think of them as being anything other than two people whom enjoyed each other in more than one way. She hopes they become a lot more than even that, but she will not hold her breathe.

As she enters into the lobby to exit the building, Javier motions her over to the receptionist's desk. She is not sure what he desires from her. No dead bodies caused by a serial killer arrived today.

She steps up to the desk as Javier states, "I know we really have not spoken about our introduction to one another at the mall, but I wanted you to know I am sorry for not properly identifying myself."

Angela feels a bit odd. Has the FBI stressed him about the day like they did Winston?

"No need to apologize. Simply an odd moment in life." replies Angela with a bright smile.

"Yes, and it seems to continue to get odder. I did not realize the man you are in a relationship with is the same man whom recently began investing in buildings to assist kids in unfortunate circumstances. I feel like a bit of an ass and am sure I looked like one to him."

Angela stops herself from giggling at Javier's expression of regret. She imagines he does feel a lower ego when comparing himself with Nicholas. She is sure many men feel inferior due to wealth and ability to do things others cannot or simply will not. She would add Nicholas's attractive physique as an ego buster, but doubts Javier is jealous of it. She did not turn away from him that day at the mall due to looks, but simply not knowing him. Looking with a more logical mind now, she must say he is not unattractive.

"Well, I am not sure if it is exactly "relationship" status. Yes, we spend time with one another and enjoy each other..."

"But have not had the talk of making it exclusive. Been there myself many a time." states Javier with a bright smile.

Angela cannot help to smile even brighter. She imagines many people know exactly what she is defining because many probably have had the same situation. How do you tell other people what you are, when you do not know exactly yourself? It is not like you demand definition with the person early on. A person does not necessarily desire to move too quickly and scare them away nor get a commitment that soon becomes their obsession and drives you crazy.

"May I ask how you realized Nicholas is the man so many are attempting to get to know? Did you attend one of his charity functions?" asks Angela.

She does not really care how he realized, but Winston has her overly paranoid about the FBI. She is not afraid of them...it is just very odd. And, she would hate for them to find out she has a relationship with Nicholas before she does. Such a thing is like your parents finding out a boy in high school likes you before you know anything about it. You simply feel like you do not really matter in the decision.

"Oh, it was really nothing. I was speaking with the FBI about the possibility of the serial killer using Nicholas as a motivation to begin killing because of the work he is doing. They agree it is a possibility. We are doing separate investigations, but assist one another."

"Wow, I am sure the extra brains on the investigation assists you immensely."

Angela watches as Javier thinks on his reply. He begins to look as if his stomach went sour. Perhaps, he does not enjoy their company.

"Well, Angela, I must say I prefer to work without them. However, they did assist me in finding a lead I never would have thought of looking into. There were photos with various bodies. The FBI sent the photos off for more professional analysis because they were able to identify the photo paper as being the kind used in developing in a dark room with real film rather than the digital way we use now."

Angela's stomach begins to churn a little. The evidence shows a black room was used. Nicholas has a black room within his home. The FBI believes the killer may have a link to Nicholas. She worries they may be correct. Though she does not know exactly who fits the position of possible killer. She only met Peter and highly doubts he is the killer. He just does not seem like the sort of person who kills people.

"I imagine you are very concerned. And, you most definitely closed in on some evidence. Not many places develop film any more."

Javier nods and replies, "Yes, only a few camera shops in town have the ability to do so. Of course, people are able to have them in their own home without us knowing, but I have another way of cutting those numbers down too."

Angela simply nods and replies, "Well, I am on my way home. Have a wonderful evening!"

"You do the same."

Angela begins to walk away only to hear the receptionist call her name. She turns back around and walks to the desk.

"This came for you after lunch. You were doing a procedure and I did not want to interrupt." states the receptionist as she hands her a large envelope.

"Thank you." replies Angela as she takes the envelope.

She looks at the handwriting on the front and knows it is from Nicholas. She cannot help smiling. She fights the urge to rip it open and read it because she feels it best to head home first. Doing so allows her to not delay whatever response she has to the envelope. If he wants to invite her over, she can simply jump in her car. If a call is desired, she can pick up the phone. Whatever it entails, she will be able to tackle it when and how she desires rather than if she reads it here. She plans to tackle it with a vengeance. And, perhaps, Nicholas too.

Chapter 31

THE EVENING AIR IS crisp as Addison walks down the street. Such an atmosphere is needed to wake him up from such a boring day. Nothing other than murder seems to go on lately. His co-workers are all about covering every angle possible and it annoys him immensely. He prefers life and celebration over death and crime.

Desiring entertainment, he enters Pick A Space to get a drink and relax. It is not his usual hangout, but will do tonight since it is so close to home. He is not exactly looking to find new friends either.

He looks around the room quickly for available seating. All booths and private tables seem full. He heads over to the bar and takes a seat in the middle of three empty bar stools. He always believes a center seat is the best choice. If someone on one side of him is a bore or annoying, he can simply talk to the person on the other side of him. And if that person is just as bad, then it will be time to leave.

"What can I get you?" asks the bartender.

"Scotch on the rocks."

In a matter of seconds, Addison has his drink and the bartender is tending someone else. Just the way Addison likes his bartenders. Do the job and walk away. He hates it when they stand there and attempt to talk with him. He always feels as if they are attempting to extort him for a bigger tip. Angela always gives him a lecture about feeling that way. However, since she is generally preoccupied with the hot Nicholas Payne lately, her words do not matter at this moment.

A man sits down on the stool to his right. His expression seems a bit intense and hateful. Addison decides to simply look forward while drinking. He does not prefer to be antisocial, but for all he knows the guy is a gay hater or serial killer. He will talk to them if they are either because his job as a reporter on society and events generally deems it so. However, he believes it best to let them decide on conversation unless it is an interview.

The bartender makes the man a whiskey sour as Addison sips his scotch. The man keeps looking around as if he is searching for someone. Addison simply continues to look ahead and drink. The man is probably searching for a date whom stood him up and he refuses to admit it.

"Anything interesting bring you here this evening?" asks the stranger before he takes a drink.

Addison looks to him and states, "Simply this nice scotch and an atmosphere with people other than just myself. How about you? I noticed you looking around. Are you expecting anyone?"

"No, just seeing who is around. A bit worried going out by myself lately."

Addison notices the guy is about done with his drink. He must have some really stressful life issues or loves some whiskey. Either way, Addison does not care to find out which of the two. He finishes his scotch and pulls out a tip for the bartender.

"Well, I hope you have a pleasant evening." states Addison as he stands up.

The man quickly finishes his drink and states, "Do you mind if I walk out with you? My car is right outside and I would feel safer if someone was there to watch me get in it."

Addison looks at the man and wonders if he is truly scared. He looks to the windows to see the street lined with vehicles.

"Yes, I walked here. It will only take me a second or two of waiting for you to enter your vehicle. Always better to be safe than sorry."

The man smiles widely and states, "Thank you."

Addison watches the man get out of his seat and they begin walking out. Yet, something does not feel right to Addison. He cannot pinpoint what feels odd about this moment, but something is a little more peculiar than he likes.

Addison holds the door open for the man so he can exit and then he follows.

"Which vehicle is yours?" asks Addison.

"This one!" yells the man as he swings around and begins punching Addison.

Blow after blow lands on Addison's body as he attempts to defend himself and swing back. After Addison is able to make a few hits himself, the man yells, "Okay boys, it is time to make this queer pay like all those other sexual deviants."

Before Addison knows who the man is directing, he hears yells all around him as punches and kicks land all over his body. He attempts to simply run away, but trips and falls to the ground. As the group begins kicking him from every direction, Addison covers his head with his arms to protect it while attempting to endure the pain. He cries out with each vicious kick and begs them to stop. Tears of pain begin to fall.

With the sound of sirens approaching, Addison hears the man state, "Okay guys, this fag has had enough. Lets get out of here."

The other men begin to run off as the man kicks Addison once again and then spits on him.

"You remember this faggot. Your kind and all those other sexual misfits are not wanted. Best leave town before our kind poses your dead body for all to see."

Addison hears the man run off in the same direction as his friends. He continues to cry from pain as the sirens get closer. He hears the bar door open and a few people rush out. As they drop to the ground to assist him, Addison simply continues to cry.

Chapter 32

AS THE BRIGHT SUN ATTEMPTS to sneak past long bedroom drapes, Angela's head rests in her palm as lays her other palm on Nicholas's chest and watches him sleep. After opening the card the night before, he whisked her away to the theater and then home to his bedroom. It was a remarkable evening she will never forget. And now, she simply examines every inch of his calm relaxed face to remember it just as much as last night.

He was either very careful as a child or very talented. She sees no childhood scars from falls or bicycle wrecks. He is very Metro-male for every hair appears perfectly in place and his eyebrows are not odd lengths. Her eyes roam down to his beautifully sculpted chest. Next to her palm are the few hairs he has in the middle of his chest. The rest is bare, except for the small strip after his belly button that leads to her wonderful enjoyment.

"Morning." whispers Nicholas as his hand rises and rests on hers.

She looks to him with a smile and says, "Morning to you too, sleepyhead. I was simply admiring the work of art you call a body."

Nicholas chuckles and states, "If you say so, but I can tell you it is not all pleasant. I am sure there is hidden fat somewhere your eyes do not allow you to see."

"Doubtful."

She feels his other arm raise and his hand pull her down to his chest. She rests her head and moves her body closer to his. She could easily fall asleep in his arms once again. However, doing so will keep them from spending awake time together, which is always better than sleeping. Yes, it is the weekend, but she still does not want to waste time sleeping when they can be out enjoying each other and the world together.

"Nicholas, should we not rise and spend the day doing remarkable things together?"

Angela feels him rub his hand up and down her back as he states, "Well, beautiful, if you simply want to return to last night all it takes is a kiss."

Angela cannot help laughing. She knows a kiss is simple enough to spark his fire. Yet, that is not the only goal she has in mind.

"Hmm, I thought perhaps a small breakfast of pastries and coffee. Followed by a rather pleasant shared shower where we can discuss further actions of the day."

"And I thought you wanted to rise much later in the day after you told Winston last night you would not be joining her in shopping today because I intended to keep you out later than you expected."

Angela raises her head and rest it back on her palm as she watches him smirking.

"Yes, I canceled with Winston. However, I am completely sure she understands why."

"I am sure she does as well."

Before she realizes his intentions, Angela is rolled on to her back as his body rests upon hers and his lips overtake her mouth. Her senses rush as his hand begins to caress her body. Perhaps she did make a mistake in suggesting breakfast.

As she enjoys the moment more and more, the phone on the nightstand rings. Nicholas stops the kissing and caressing as he drops his head into the pillow next to her head. She believes he wants to avoid the distraction as much as she does not want it, which is easily remedied.

Running her hands down his back, she states, "Just ignore it." and kisses his neck.

Nicholas pops his head up and rolls away from her as he states, "I cannot. The only person with this number is my lawyer. Unfortunately, when he calls, it is generally very important and cannot be ignored."

As Nicholas answers the phone, Angela rests on her side with head in palm once again.

"Okay, but how did you get this number?" asks Nicholas.

Angela is unable to hear the answer nor does she really care. She wants to return to what they were doing.

With a confused expression, Nicholas turns around and hands her the phone as he states, "The call is for you. It is Winston and she says it is very important."

Angela cautiously takes the phone and says, "Hello?"

"Angela, I hate interrupting whatever it is you are doing, but something very bad has happened to Addison."

Angela's heart sinks as she asks, "Is Addie alright? What happened?"

"Well, he went out for a drink last night at Pick A Place. It ended with him being beaten by several people because he is gay. They instructed him to stop being gay or he will end up being posed like the serial killer's victims. He is at St. John's Hospital with some broken ribs and a lot of bruising."

Angela feels the tears run down her cheeks as she states, "Thank you, Winston. I will be at the hospital soon."

She hands the phone back to Nicholas and watches him hang up. Sure he does not care to hear her internal pain, she jumps out of bed and begins searching for her clothes.

"Angela, what is going on?"

With tears continuously rolling down her cheeks, Angela looks to him and states, "Some gay bashers assaulted Addison last night and now he is in the hospital."

Nicholas rushes over to her and wraps his arms around her. Angela looses all of the control of the sorrow she was withholding and the tears begin to become a resemblance of Niagara Falls.

"It is okay. I will go to the hospital with you."

With those simple words, Angela feels closer to Nicholas than she has anyone. Her eyes begin to dry a bit as she remains in his arms and realizes she is falling for him faster than ever intended. She adores it, but it scares her a bit too.

Chapter 33

JAVIER STEPS OUT OF his vehicle and looks at the Payne mansion. He is truly impressed and understands completely how he was able to snag the beautiful Angela. Not only is the size of the home impressive, but the gardening surrounding the home definitely displays talent. Yet, he doubts Mr. Payne is the creation of the beauty. Why would he? His money can do it for him.

"Are we admiring the home all day? Or, are we eventually knocking on the door?" asks Steve.

Javier glares at him as he begins walking towards the front doors. His heart is beating faster than he wants. Though it is not the house nor gardening it causing it to happen.

The last time he was in Mr. Payne's presence, the man managed to sneak off with Angela and totally interrupted his play on scoring a date. He technically lost to this man. However, they were not really competing. So, he will try to calm his heart and not hold it against Mr. Payne. After all he is attempting to do with his organizations, Javier knows he needs to respect him at least a little bit.

Once they reach the doors, Steve rings the door bell as Javier takes out his badge for presentation. He doubts it will intimidate Mr. Payne, but maybe it will take the man's ego down just a bit.

The door opens and an unknown man appears. He simply looks back and forth at Javier and Steve. No, hello or can I help you. Simply an inquisitive expression.

"Hello, I am Detective Javier Alexander. My partner, Detective Steve Olsen, and I are here to meet with Mr. Payne." states Javier as he flashes his badge.

The man smiles wide and states, "Please come in." and opens the door for them to enter.

As they enter the home, Javier continues to look around. This is his first time in such a large estate. Hell, it is probably his last time too.

"Please wait here. I will notify Nicholas of your arrival."

Javier watches the man hurry off down a hallway. He wishes the man would at least identify himself prior to departing the room. Javier hates not knowing people's names.

"Who do you think that guy is? Butler? Housekeeper?" asks Steve.

"I have no idea. However, I intend to find out everyone connected to Mr. Payne." whispers Javier. "You cannot tell me he is not the inspiration of this killer."

Steve simply nods as Javier continues to look around. The interior of the home is just as wonderful as the outer appearance. The foyer holds a few antiques and pieces of artwork. Each piece is attractive and interesting without standing out over the other pieces. Javier wonders if an interior designer chose the pieces or if Mr. Payne is educated in decorating.

"Welcome, gentlemen. If you do not mind, I prefer to talk in my library. The room is generally the place I meet anyone when it is of a formal nature, but not business oriented." states Nicholas from the top of the stairs.

Javier and Steve look up as Javier replies, "Of course. Happy to oblige."

Javier finds Nicholas's statement a bit odd considering they believe his foundations are causing the killer to kill. Are the foundations not business oriented?

As Javier and Steve walk to the staircase, Javier attempts to keep an eye on Mr. Payne while making it look as if he is still simply looking around. A very tricky movement when he has already looked over the area completely.

Reaching the top, Javier offers his hand and states, "Happy to meet with you once again. I am sure this will be much longer and more positive than the last time we met."

"I am sure it may end in such a manner." states Nicholas as he shakes both men's hands.

Without stating another word, Nicholas turns around and motions to the men to follow him as he begins walking. Javier wonders if this will actually end on a positive note. The man seems disturbed about something. Yet, Javier cannot imagine what would agitate this man. He has money, a large house, servants and the beautiful Angela. What on earth can be so wrong? It is not like he is the one chasing around a serial killer that is great at hiding his tracks.

As they pass a door, Javier notices a sign stating Dark Room. He simply stops in the hallway and stares.

"Is something wrong?" asks Steve.

"Mr. Payne, just a quick question. How long have you had a dark room? Are you trained in photography?"

Javier quickly looks to Nicholas and waits for an answer. The man turns around slowly with a blank expression. As he begins walking towards the door, Nicholas states, "I do not have a dark room within my home. The room was established as one very far back in time. Once I moved in, I changed the status of the room, but left the sign for nostalgia purposes."

Javier watches him open the door and motion for them to enter. Simply stepping to the doorway and looking into the room, Javier understands the stupidity of the question. The room consists of various games from wall to wall. Video games, pin ball machines, darts and a pool table all hold a place within. There is even a Skeeball game and air hockey in a corner area of the large room. All arcade fanatics dream of owning such a room.

Javier simply turns around and nods at Nicholas. They begin walking down the hall once again as Javier places his ego a bit more in check. This is the second time this man has made him feel like an idiot. He hates to think it is the man's talent, but it truly feels like it.

At almost the end of the hallway, Nicholas turns to the left and opens a door. Rather than having his guests enter first, he simply enters and continues walking to his desk. Javier does a quick scan of the room prior to taking a seat in the chairs Nicholas motions them to sit in. The room is filled with books. Yet, the only other item it adorns is his desk and the two chairs in front of it. Javier finds it a bit odd. He refers to the room as a library even though it seems more an office. Perhaps, Mr. Payne is too uptight to relax with a good book sitting in a chair next to the fire place.

"I do hope to make this discussion a bit quick. There are things I need to address today." states Nicholas.

"Of course, Mr. Payne." vows Javier. "I am sure your attorney explained we simply believe our local serial killer may have found inspiration upon your arrival to our town. The killings all seem to have the same motive."

"Possible. Yet, I doubt it. Tell me, what motive are you assigning to the killer? The news people always seem to fail to mention one."

"You must not watch the news lately. They plaster it throughout the story now." states Steve.

Javier watches Nicholas shrug.

"All the killings are based on adults whom violated someone else in a sexual nature. Since you are working on opening housing for emancipated children, we believe the killer found motivation in protecting children, such as emancipated ones, from a major problem."

"Possible."

Javier nods as he wonders why Nicholas is so short in conversation. The man has several organizations requiring fundraisers. So, the man can influence people. Yet, right now, he seems to say nothing. If someone was attempting to protect the kids Javier wanted to protect, then he would sure be more entertaining than this. Perhaps, the man believes it is all beneath his stature.

"We worry the killer is some how linked to one of your operations or yourself." states Javier.

Seeing the anger form in Nicholas's eyes, Javier quickly says, "I do not mean as in your right hand man or a person working in your organizations. I simply mean the killer may have some sort of connection. The killings began before most people ever knew you were living here or about your organizations. Which leads me to believe, the killer connected with your lifestyle close to the beginning of your arrival."

Javier watches Nicholas calm a bit and begin to tap his fingers. He hates it when people tap their fingers.

"You make sense. However, I fail to see what you exactly desire from me."

Javier smiles and politely asks, "Can we speak with your employees?"

Nicholas laughs and states, "I doubt any of them will speak with you for about all of them are ex-convicts. And those that are not, had a parent who was a convict, which caused them to grow up in foster care. The police are generally not the people they like to speak with on any matter."

Javier simply stares at Nicholas as Steve pleads, "Please allow us to simply know whom works for you. Chances are the killer is simply someone your employees know from life. We are not stating they are responsible in any way. We just need to know who your employees are so we can talk with our street officers and learn about personal associations. Someone spoke of you in a good manner that has caused a killer."

"Yes, well, the press spoke of the killer, which inspired some gay haters to assault my girlfriend's friend. Are the gay haters on your list to find?"

Javier now understands Nicholas's attitude. He heard about the incident last night, but did not realize it was a friend of Angela's. He hates to hear about things like that happening, but is glad he can argue with Steve a little bit more about the thugs being just asses and not partnering up with the killer for their crime was not committed against a predator. They simply hate gays for being gay, which pisses Javier off more than the serial killer.

"We have people out looking for them as we speak. A video recording from across the street managed to get some of their faces." replies Javier. "As I stated, we do not believe anyone you rely on is designing the murders. They simply may know someone who is either the killer or knows the killer."

"I will get a list of those working for me and submit it to my lawyer. He can decide what is acceptable for you to know or not know."

Rather than debate particulars, Javier stands as he states, "Thank you, Mr. Payne. We look forward to hearing from him. We will see ourselves out. Please have a wonderful day."

Javier simply turns away and begins walking as Steve races up to him. They exit the library and begin down the hall when Steve asks, "Does he seem a little high strung to you?"

Javier shrugs and replies, "We do not know everything he is dealing with today. However, I do intend to know a bit more than he wants to tell me."

Chapter 34

NICHOLAS SITS AT HIS dining table as Peter enters the room with a cart and begins clearing off the dirty plates. He simply watches Peter and wonders how long he, himself, has sat there in thought. He was done with his meal and lost himself in thinking of the terrible day he has had. Peter, obviously, understands he is done and simply attempts to finish up so he can return home. Yet, Nicholas feels a need to connect with him about life.

"Peter, can I ask you something?"

As he continues to load the cart, Peter states, "Yes and I have something to tell you as well."

Nicholas is a bit shocked at the reply. He doubts it is anything of huge importance. However, maybe, Angela left a message with him while Nicholas was out meeting with his lawyer.

"How likely do you think it is the police will attempt some sort of observation of me and the people whom work for me?"

Peter looks at him with the eyes of an owl and simply stares. Nicholas knows he believes the thought ridiculous, but Nicholas is not so sure it is. The police went through his lawyer to talk to him and then came demanding private information from him. His lawyer did inform him they had no right to the information without a warrant, which was likely not obtainable. Yet, Nicholas does not think this is the end of their attempt.

"Peter, I know you find the question odd. However, with their recent requests, I cannot help thinking on it because it will give them the information they need without obtaining a warrant."

"Nicholas, you stress too much. Even if they begin to watch you, they will simply record names of those whom you talk to and follow those routes."

Nicholas shakes his head and states, "No, they may see a bit more."

Once again, those owl eyes are on him. Nicholas wishes he would not do it. The whole image is simply odd.

"What possibly could they see to cause you so much stress? If it is the live porno of you making love to Angela, I am sure your lawyer will find a way to sue?" states Peter.

Nicholas laughs and replies, "Oh, I am sure it would end with more than a lawsuit. As for fear, I am a bit worried about them finding me of doing something illegal I feel should not be illegal."

"Are you hinting to me you have been smoking some Mary Jane and did not bother to share? If so, then you are a bit stupid because I am sure I have connections to better quality and a lower price tag."

Nicholas rolls his eyes. He should have thought more about this subject before bringing it up to Peter. The man is renowned at not participating in a conversation by talking. He will say millions of things and none of it is part of the conversation you attempt to make. Best to just drop it and talk about something else.

"What is it you need to inform me about?"

Peter's face lights up as he states, "My connections paid off. I finally found someone familiar with the existence of Angela's brother."

Nicholas was not expecting to hear that. Angela will be excited.

"Where is he? Is he still alive?" asks Nicholas.

Peter shakes his head and replies, "Patience, monsieur. I told you I found someone whom knew the boy existed. He also saw him face to face once, but was long ago."

Nicholas feels his excitement plummet. He doubts this person will be of any help. Seeing a person once and long ago does not mean the person is able to track the man down.

"Peter, are you sure the person can help? I do not want to tell Angela and it lead to nothing."

With the last plate on the cart, Peter replies, "Now, you are really getting ahead of reality. I told you about finding this person simply so you are aware I am still working on finding the brother. Mentioning it to Angela is absolutely stupid since we have no idea where this may lead."

Nicholas believes the day may have been too much for him because Peter's words simply feel as if he is running in circles. Perhaps, he should call it a day...

"Now, you are aware of the person I found, simply sit back and wait until I can tell you more. The man may find out more when talking with someone, he may find the brother or find nothing. You simply need to keep it to yourself and wait to find out." demands Peter.

Slightly angered at the directions, Nicholas replies, "Since your such a wonderful fount of information, why do you not find out who attacked Angela's friend, Addison, for me too?"

Nicholas watches Peter simply stare at him. He knows Peter attempts to figure out how serious he is about the question. And he is happy to explain he is very serious if Peter will simply ask the question. Yet, he knows Peter is probably putting him in check for asking so snidely.

"What do you plan to do with information like that? Are you looking to build a vigilante lifestyle? Or, perhaps hire someone to do it for you? I hate to think you search for it to buy off the police from watching you because it will not work. Things like that never work."

Nicholas understands why he questions why he asks. The last thing Peter wants is a connection to something capable of landing him back in prison. Realizing his limitations on conversation, Nicholas replies, "No, Peter, nothing like any of those things. It was a sarcastic comment meant to annoy you. Though, I would like to see those people face our legal system. What they did to Addison is wrong and the fact they threatened him with the so called serial killer is moronic."

"Now, some may disagree with you. NO ONE you or I would converse with about life among society will state such a thing. However, you take up the conversation with some holier than though individuals whom need to study their bible a bit more, you may find yourself arguing."

Nicholas looks to the ground because he knows Peter is correct. He feels most of society is for allowing everyone to live their life and be happy. Yet, there are always those few whom want everybody to follow what they deem is right.

"I am sure there are those who will disagree. I know you faced disagreement about life choices as well and you seem perfectly fine. Do you think I am unable to handle it?"

Peter chuckles and takes a seat. He looks to Nicholas and states, "You are a strong man, Nicholas. However, you are a person whom generally only associates for a reason. Whether it is to raise funds, help someone out, employ someone or even romance the beautiful Angela, the relationship always has a reason. So you may not be able to handle it as a normal individual because conversing with the person has limitations in order for the relationship to last and serve its purpose. Unlike myself, you need things to go a specific way in order for the relationship, which in some way you need, to continue. Your life consists of limiting your self expression."

"Peter, a lot of people do. You cannot say everything you desire anytime you want."

"Nicholas, yes, you can. How many times have you trapped me in answering a question? Admit it, not once. Why? Because I do not impose limits on myself for the sake of others. I tell you my thoughts on what I desire to tell you and nothing more. Doing so, keeps me in control of me and others from getting closer than I desire. Life like mine teaches you to do so."

"There are things I hide as well." retorts Nicholas.

"Everyone does hide things, Nicholas. However, as I said before, you are required to keep connections with people. All I meet, including yourself, is not of importance to me. Please do not take offense. I simply learned in order for my life to go right, I need to keep control by keeping people at a distance, worrying about myself and never give anyone the ability to hold something over my head with demands. I learned to live my life for me."

Nicholas sees the tension in his eyes and knows Peter is very serious about the matter. He does not take offense to Peter's words because he does not care to control his life. He thinks their relationship is perfect. Yet, he will not state so because... Well, after Peter said what he just stated, Nicholas may need to watch what he states to the man simply to feel on the same social level.

"Perhaps you are right, Peter." states Nicholas as he rises and walks out of the room.

Nicholas is not sure where he wants to go in the house. Hell, he is not sure if he wants to stay in the house at this moment. He wishes Angela had left the hospital to see him, but her mind is set on Addison at the moment.

Perhaps a trip to the house in the wooded area will release some of his stress. He has not looked through his files for a bit. Finding an error in operation and doing away with it shall release a bit of stress as well as make life easier.

Chapter 35

ANGELA WALKS DOWN A coroner's office hallway and attempts to keep her eyes from everyone. She does not really have anything to hide other than the stress of what happened to Addie. The damage to his body was pretty bad, but thankfully, he lived through the attack. She hates to think of how she would be if he had not.

Now, Addie is recovering and she can continue on with life. Well, she can continue after she meets with Javier and his partner, which is where she is headed. She is not too sure what the meeting is about nor why Winston is not in attendance. So, she imagines they simply want to discuss what happened to Addison with her. After all, the group did reference the serial killer after attacking him, which to her is idiotic because a serial killer kills instead of beating people. If those people had any brains, they would realize the difference and stop attempting to act like someone they are not.

Angela turns to the right and enters the conference room. Steve and Javier are already seated. Javier turns his head towards her and states, "Hello, Angela. Please close the door and take a seat."

Not desiring a false representation of her emotions at the moment, she refuses to give the "expected" smile and simply does as he asked. She hopes it does not offend either of the gentlemen. She simply does not desire to display a false persona right now.

After she takes a seat, Angela takes a deep breath and asks, "What do you need to talk with me about? I assume it is about the attack on my friend, Addison, since Winston is not part of this meeting."

Both men slowly look at one another as Steve asks, "You are close friends with the recent assault victim?"

"Yes, he has been my friend for years."

Javier knows he already knows the answer to Steve's question, but asking it anyway may allow her to let go of her apparent torment from the incident. He does not like seeing her this way.

Javier shakes his head and states, "Angela, other officers are investigating the assault because we do not feel it is connected to the murders. Very sorry to hear about your friend and wish him a fast recovery."

Angela is not sure what the meeting is about now unless they want to have another medical professional do the autopsies. If so, she really does not care because the individual she works on does not exactly matter to her. She simply likes to find out why each person died.

"I am not sure what you want to speak to me about then. Do you have a question on one of the autopsies?"

Javier smiles and replies, "No, to be honest we simply want to ask you a few questions about Nicholas Payne. We think the killer is using him for inspiration much like the people whom assaulted Winston used the killer for inspiration. So we simply are looking at Nicholas's lifestyle to find out his connections to the public."

Well, talking about Nicholas will surely bring a happy light into her day. However, she is not sure why they simply do not ask him for he knows more about his life than she does.

"I am not sure about how much assistance I will be. Why do you not speak with Nicholas?"

With a tight smile, Steve replies, "We attempted to do so, which led to long conversation with his lawyer and a tight lipped Nicholas Payne."

"We do not want to disrupt his life nor the life of those working for him. We simply want to understand who sees him and has connections with those whom work for him." interjects Javier.

Angela understands how difficult it may be for them to find out the information they desire. Nicholas is not a big talker on things occurring in his life. Though she cannot really brag on revealing all either. Perhaps, it is the reason they connect so well.

"Well, I can answer questions, but I feel you will be disappointed with the knowledge I have." replies Angela with a giggle.

Javier smiles and asks, "Do you know any of the people working within his home? We met one man when visiting him. Yet, we failed to get a name or his actual job."

Steve states, "His lawyer told us he employed a chef, a cleaning staff and a landscaping crew. All of the people are ex-convicts."

Angela suddenly feels deprived of Nicholas's life. How did she ever forget to ask such questions? Obviously, the estate is too large for Peter to do all the work and Nicholas is not completing it.

"Wow, I failed to learn a large bit of information concerning the operation of the household. The conversation of who cleans or landscapes the home never took place between us. The chef is a man named Peter. I have met him. He is very nice."

Angela sees Steve jotting notes and begins to feel a bit nervous. She did not really supply any information other than Peter's name, but she begins to wonder if she should tell them anything.

Javier asks, "Do they have a good relationship?"

"From what I have seen they get along very well. Peter works on getting Nicholas to eat properly, which causes Nicholas to taunt him a bit with jokes, but Peter never seems to care what he states."

Javier nods and looks at Steve. He seems to have run out of questions.

"Have you heard them mention names about people coming to do something such as cleaning or lawn mowing? Perhaps, seen a picture of staff laying around the home?" asks Steve in a rather negative tone.

Angela is not sure if the man is naturally mean or if she should start to get offended. Rather than take it offensively, she states, "No, I never heard them discuss anything concerning the home nor seen pictures of anyone. Though I have seen a door stating Dark Room. Whether Nicholas practices photography or not has never been discussed either."

Javier laughs and states, "We can assure you he does not practice photography. I asked about the room on our visit. Upon moving in, he transformed the room into an arcade. About every game in existence is there. You should ask him about it. I am sure you will enjoy it."

Angela giggles as she looks at Javier. She feels a bit jealous Javier knows something she does not. However, she has not had a problem getting Nicholas to talk to her. So, neither of them have an advantage.

"Well, I believe you answered all we have to ask you about. Thank you." states Steve.

Angela watches Javier glare at him as he states, "Let me get the door for you."

Angela meets Javier at the door as he opens it. He gives her a bright smile as she walks out of the room.

After a few seconds of her walking away, he shuts the door and asks Steve, "Did something crawl up your ass? Why get so negative in the questioning?"

Rather than look at him and answer, Steve continues writing down something and states, "I thought another tone may cause her to get more friendly with you."

Javier knows he is being sarcastic, which angers him a bit.

Steve looks to him and states, "Look, Javier, it was obvious she does not know anything about the operation of the household. And, why would she? I doubt they find a need to discuss it."

"Yes, but there is no reason to get mean."

Steve begins tapping his pen on his notepad. Javier hates the sound just as much as watching someone tap their fingers on a table.

"A thought came into my head about one of Mr. Payne's answers when you were discussing the dark room. He stated he did not have a dark room within his home rather than state he did not have a dark room. Is it possible the home is the wrong place to be looking for information?"

"You have a point." replies Javier as he sits down. "You think we simply look at the wrong location to find the information we need?"

Javier watches Steve nod with a smile. For once, he actually agrees with the man. The reply is a bit odd. Either you have a dark room or you do not. Why state you do not have one in your home?

"Where do you think we need to begin our new search? The man has a lot of money. We know he owns three buildings. Do we need to search through property listings and find out exactly all he owns in town?"

Steve shakes his head and replies, "No, I think our first target to talk is this Peter guy. I have a feeling he is the man who answered the door. He did not seem confident in answering the door nor did he choose to escort us to Mr. Payne instead of notifying him of our arrival, which means he is more than likely familiar with limited areas of the house. If he is a chef, then his prime locations are the kitchen and dining room."

"Very perceptive, Steve. I am rather impressed with your logic on this one. How do you believe we should begin talks with Peter? We do not know anything about him other than where he works. Being an ex-convict, he may not really desire to talk to us. Especially, if he sees talking to us as a threat to his job."

And overly large grin crosses Steve's face as he replies, "We are not going to address him about talking to us."

"We aren't?"

Steve shakes his head and replies, "No, you are going to have a conversation with either Angela or Winston about asking him to talk to us. He is familiar with them and will trust their request rather than our request. Though I prefer Angela asking him since she has already talked with us and can share her experience."

Javier is a bit unsure of addressing the man this way. Yes, he probably will trust them more than detectives, but he is unsure about the women asking because if the killer manages to find out, she will be at risk.

"How do you know he would talk with Winston about talking with us?"

Steve shrugs and states, "When talking with her, she told me about having lunch there with Angela. He apparently slipped her his phone number after she asked him a question."

"What question?"

"I do not know. She would not tell me, but she stated it was more of a business conversation than personal."

Javier finds that very odd. He doubts it has anything to do with the murders. Yet, he cannot see the reasoning of not answering the question. If it was a business conversation, then no reason to hide the conversation.

"I find that whole scenario a bit odd. I will talk with Angela about speaking with Peter. She has been there more than Winston and is more familiar with the man."

"Are you sure you are not allowing your ego to decide for you? I mean you two do seem a lot more cordial to one another than in the beginning." Steve says jokingly.

Javier sneers at him and rises from his chair. He is not even going to respond to such a question. The last thing he needs is Steve concentrating on their interactions with one another rather than the case. Though, he must admit, they are a bit nicer to one another now.

"I am going to go talk to Angela. You stay hear with your negative attitude and tap away in frustration. By the way, I am about to make sure you never have a pen in your hand again during questioning."

Without waiting for a reply, Javier opens the door and exits the room. He is pretty sure Angela is beginning an autopsy by now. So, he will simply ask the receptionist for her phone number and call her later. Calling later will allow her to cool off from Steve's negative attitude. Though, it may also place her with Mr. Payne during the call. He is not sure if he will like asking her to do it then. He does not care if Mr. Payne knows...well, yes, he does a bit. Primarily, though, he just rather she not be with Mr. Payne.

Chapter 36

AS THE BRIGHT SUN BEGINS to descend from the sky, Simone Blickwell watches neighborhood kids play while sitting on his front porch. They all scurry about and run across the front lawns in a game of tag.

Watching them is nothing new for him. They always seem to attract his attention whether through words they shout at one another or actions when playing. Unlike adults, they all have their own way of analyzing things and dealing with whatever appears before them. He always finds it fascinating.

Not desiring anymore inspiration, Simone grabs his glass of wine and retreats into his home. The entertainment outside shall all return home soon for the street lights are about to come on. Heaven forbid a child walk home in the dark on a lighted street. Simone laughs and shakes his head as he heads to his kitchen to refill his wine glass.

He enters his kitchen and sees his cat resting on the counter.

"Mr. Precious, you know you are not supposed to be up there."

The cat half lowers his eyes and opens them again. Simone ignores the response as he reaches into his refrigerator and pulls out the wine. He sets his glass on the counter and uncorks the bottle. As he is pouring, he states, "Mr. Precious, I know you do not believe yourself a threat to anything while laying on my counter. However, science tells me otherwise. Your making me decide between you and scientific data. I do not believe you have the evidence they do to support your reasoning."

Mr. Precious meows as he re-corks the bottle and places it in the refrigerator. Simone takes a sip of wine while he looks at Mr. Precious as he begins purring.

"Fine, Mr. Precious, you can lay there right now, but only because I plan on cleaning the kitchen tomorrow anyways. Tomorrow evening you shall find another location, understand?"

Simone turns and walks away towards his living room on the lower floor. The windowless room shall once again give him the comfort of nighttime even though it is simply late afternoon. His years of staying out all night in his youth cause him to miss the darkness. Now, people constantly desire it to be daytime. They put timers on lights throughout their home so darkness is never seen. Or, they buy those daytime light bulbs to make the light look as if the sun is lighting the room. To him, it is all a waste. Darkness offers so much more than light. With darkness, you can surprise you enemy, hide from stalkers, sneak touches with another and so much more.

Simone picks the remote up off the table and turns on the television. The bright light basks through the dark room. Simone is suddenly able to see a man standing behind his couch. He jumps a bit and yells, "Who are you? What are you doing in my home?"

Simone watches the man as he simply looks around the room. There is something familiar about him, but Simone is not sure why he seems familiar.

"I ask once again, who are you? Are you on drugs?"

Simone watches the man break into laughter and then he replies, "No, Simone, I am not on drugs. I have always stayed away from drugs. Remember, you told me drugs were the thing to kill me. Nothing we were to do was to kill me. Just the use of drugs. Remember that?"

Simone takes a deep breathe for he realizes the man is one of the kids from times past. He is not sure exactly which one, but he knows what he said and what was done. Simone responds, "Since you remember me, tell me your name. It is common courtesy to help one another remember each other."

Simone sees an anger cross the man's face as he quickly points a taser and launches the attack. Simone feels electricity run through his body as he falls to the floor and yells "stop". As he continuously cries out in pain, the man walks around the couch and stands next to his body. The voltage stops as the man squats down next to him.

Afraid of what the man may do next, but unable to rise from the floor quickly, Simone simply keeps a hard grasp on the wine glass in his hand as he asks, "Are you him? Are you the killer the news keeps talking about? The one who is building an army."

The man punches him in the stomach and replies, "Those haters do not live by my theory of proper human life. I will be sure to send a message out about the matter."

With the answer, Simone knows the man is the killer and intends to make him pay for his sins with children. Since the volts are not running through his body and ache of the punch lowers a bit, Simone knows he must act quickly if he desires to live.

Realizing the man is still squatting and close enough, Simone quickly slams the wine glass against the side of the man's face and attempts to rise off the floor. Nearly to a standing position, Simone once again feels the electric charge run through his body and screams in agony.

"Wow, I guess you did teach your brain to forget pain as it travels through your body. Too bad you never taught us to forget anything."

The voltage stops and Simone begins to cry. He knows he is not going to be able to break away from this man. He prays somebody hears what is going on and calls the police.

"Now, tears are not the camera's friend. The crowd does not like tears nor the sound of crying. Remember?"

The volts once again begin bursting through every inch of him. As every muscle in his body feels the electrical torment, Simone knows his luck has finally run out. Tonight, he shall die and it will be one of the children he once filmed writing his ending.

The voltage stops once again and Simone muscles the little energy he has to ask, "Why not just kill me now? Why prolong it?"

All emotion seems to wash away from the man's face as he questions, "Why? How can you not realize?"

Simone simply shakes his head no. He has no idea what the man is thinking and simply wants to die.

"The damage you have done to all of us children did not end by us no longer being in your picture shows. The memories of the fear, pain, awkwardness and everything else did not end. Why should yours?"

The electric charge rips through Simone once again. He knows this is the end. This is the finale of his life. As cries of agony venture out of his throat, he simply wonders when it will be all over.

Chapter 37

"HELLO, NICHOLAS, I am here visiting Addie, but intend to leave soon. I was hoping to connect with you since it has been a few days. Hopefully, see you soon. Goodbye."

Angela hangs up the phone and looks to Addie's disappointed expression. She is pretty confident she displays the same expression. Ever since the attack, her days seem to have been simply work and looking after Addie after the hospital sent him home. She stayed with him for a bit since he was still in a bit of pain as well as scared to stay alone. Then, this morning, Addie called her at work and told her this evening was her final visitation to the sick. Apparently, Addie felt she babies him too much and demands she get a social life.

"Doll, I am sure he shall jump with joy on hearing your message. He simply is not home yet." states Addison.

Angela giggles and prays he is right. God, she cannot wait to see him again. It has only been a few days, but feels like an eternity.

"I am sure you are right, Addie. Before I go, can I ask you about something?"

"Shoot away."

Angela takes a seat on the couch next to him. She is not sure how to start the conversation without seeming to be exactly what she attempts to not be.

"I told you Javier and Steve spoke to me about your attack and how another division was looking into your case."

Addie simply nods.

"I did not tell you all of the conversation. They asked if I can do something for them."

"What on earth are those idiots attempting to lure you into? You are not a detective."

Angela takes a deep breath and replies, "They are not attempting to get me involved in anything, really. Javier believes the killer is finding inspiration from Nicholas. They are attempting to find out more about his life to see possible connections. Unfortunately, Nicholas and his lawyer do not desire to inform them about the people working for him, which I understand completely."

Addison reaches for his drink and asks, "Then, why are we having this conversation? If you understand Nicholas, then you have to agree giving them information is crossing the line Nicholas does not want crossed."

She watches Addie take a drink. Perhaps, he is right. Will Nicholas feel betrayed if she simply asks Peter to talk to Javier? An even better question, will Peter tell Nicholas she asked him to do it?

"Your scaring me, Addie. I am not attempting to cause any harm in Nicholas's relationship with me nor with his staff. I only ask you to help me figure this out so hopefully Javier finds the information he needs and stops the madness going on."

Feeling the formation of tears, Angela bites her lips and looks to the floor. She hates looking someone face-to-face when her eyes are about to spring a leak. And, she has no idea why the tears are even forming. She has not done anything wrong yet.

"Angela, if Javier simply wants you to ask Peter to speak to him simply mention it to the man and be done with it."

"I think I fear what may happen simply by asking. Peter is very nice and humorous. Yet, I do not really know the man nor do I really get left alone with him to ask him in private. I only see him when he serves the meals to Nicholas and I."

Feeling she has her emotions in check after admitting her lack of connection, Angela looks to Addie as he takes a drink. She expects him to look annoyed, but he seems calm as any day, which is good because it means he is actually thinking on what she said.

"You simply need to play it as any other day. When a brief moment of whisper is available, ask Peter. Other than that, drop it. The last thing you need to do is ask a bunch of ex-convicts to talk the police. I am not one and I rarely desire to talk to the police."

Angela giggles and asks, "What about the one you met on the cruise in the Bahamas? You seemed to like talking to him."

Addie glares at her and replies, "You know I enjoyed a lot more with him than simply talking. Wish he was here now, but he simply could not walk away from living in New Jersey."

With a bright smile, Angela replies, "Okay, well, I am going to head on home. Your sure everything is okay for the evening? You do not need anything?"

"Angela, leave before I begin throwing things and shouting."

Angela wiggles her fingers goodbye and heads for the door. As she walks out of it and shuts the door, she prays Addie remains safe, but knows she is getting a little too fearful. The attack happened at the bar, not his home. Though the bar is not far from home...

She checks to make sure the door locked behind her. Unable to twist the knob, she feels a weight lift off of her. Now, her only prayers are Addie remains home and Nicholas finds her. Or, at least, calls her to talk about absolutely nothing.

She looks up and down the street as she gets in her car to make sure no one odd is watching her. The last thing she needs is to fight for her own life. Locking the doors and turning on the ignition, Angela tries to think of something other than Nicholas. She imagines the conversation with Addie in combination with the message she left has her brain programmed to think of only him.

Driving down the road, she turns on the radio in attempt to drop the thought of him. She will not be able to sleep tonight if she does not clear him from her brain. She hates when it happens. Though, she has not done it since high school puppy love. Maybe she is past all of that happening now. Lord, she prays she is.

As Angela parks her vehicle, she notices a limosine parked in front of her building with a driver standing on the passenger side waiting to open the door. Someone must be celebrating something special.

After exiting her car, Angela walks past the driver and says, "Hello.". She continues walking and turns to go up the front steps.

"Madame, I think you are mistaken on thinking I wait for another individual. The limosine is for you on behalf of Mr. Nicholas Payne. You are Miss Angela Summers, are you not?"

Angela quickly turns around and replies, "Yes, I am Angela Summers. Is Nicholas in the limosine?"

"No, madame, he arranged for me to take you to him. If you need time to do anything, I will wait patiently."

Angela feels as if the ground she is standing on just swept away from her. Nicholas does not bother to return her message, but sends a limosine to whisk her away to him. She wonders where he is located. Is he at home? Or, at some extraordinary hotel with a penthouse suite? She does not care whether he is at one or the other. She simply wants to see him.

Angela states, "No, I am ready to leave now.", as she walks towards the limosine. The driver opens the door and she takes a seat.

As the driver makes his way to the driver's seat, she looks around at the exquisite leather and posh floor covering. Definitely a high end vehicle even in limosine standards. Now, she simply needs to think of a way to thank Nicholas.

Chapter 38

AS A SLIVER OF SUNLIGHT manages to shine through heavy ornate curtains, Angela opens her eyes. She takes a deep breath while she wonders if Nicholas still sleeps next to her. She does not feel his body touching hers. Yet, he still may be in bed since it is a rather large bed.

She simply roles over to see if he is there so she can possibly snuggle up to him. Her excitement drops just a bit when she realizes she is the only one in the bed. Oh well, last night was amazing and she is sure today will grow into a positive journey with him.

She cannot remember any man sweeping her off her feet like Nicholas. After the limosine brought her to his home, she was greeted with a wonderful kiss. She expected for them to simply head to the bedroom on her arrival. Instead, he took her to the Dark Room to play some games, which led to a game of strip darts. She never really thought the game existed, but Nicholas proved her wrong. And, she is so thankful for his ability in getting things right where they are meant to go.

Angela rises out of bed and walks towards Nicholas's closet. He told her last night to pick out whatever she likes to wear until he can take her home for a change of clothes. He laughed at her for forgetting to bring some. She was a little embarrassed about her desire sparking her to rush off without thinking of the next day. However, Nicholas made up for laughing simply by stating he would return her home briefly so she can change into her own clothes. He obviously wants to see her today as well. The word briefly never meant so much to her as it does now.

After simply throwing on a pair of athletic shorts and a plain t-shirt, Angela rushes out of the room and down the hall. She wants to find Nicholas. However, her stomach is beginning to growl. So, her first destination is the kitchen to grab something simple to eat. She is not sure if Peter is there to make her something. So, even a few pieces of cheese and some grapes shall make her happy.

As she nears the kitchen, she hears the movement of pans and cooking utensils, which means Peter is there or Nicholas has become creative in the kitchen. Doubting the latter, she enters the kitchen and is welcomed with a smile from Peter.

"Good morning, princess. I am making this wonderful crepe for you and was going to deliver it to you in bed, but since you came down, you can eat it here."

Angela smiles and replies, "Sounds and smells wonderful."

Angela walks over to a kitchen stool and takes a seat at the counter. Peter throws some strawberries in a sauce he made and stirs it around to heat it up. She wonders what is in the crepe since he already rolled it. Watching him pour the sauce with strawberries over the crepe, her mouth begins to water. He then spoons out a bit of whipped cream from a nearby bowl and places it on top.

As he slides the plate to her and hands her a fork, Peter states, "Start on this and I will make my way to the refrigerator to get you a drink. Any morning preference?"

Staring at her wonderful morning treat, Angela simply replies, "Coke."

She hears Peter laugh and is sure he does not hear the request often. She takes a bite of her breakfast. As the flavoring rushes through her mouth, she simply wants to take bigger bites. The cream cheese filling is unbelievable. She so wants to give Peter a hug simply to show how much she enjoys his creation.

Peter places a Coke and a chilled glass in front of her plate, but she ignores it. She finds the breakfast too tasteful to interrupt with a drink.

Before taking another bite, she asks, "Peter, is Nicholas here?"

"No, princess, he needed to visit one of his buildings today. He told me to tell you he will not be long though. He simply needs to speak with the security system people prior to installation."

Angela pours her Coke into her chilled glass and takes a drink. She is sure Nicholas's meeting is very important, but wonders how involved he is with his operations. By no means is she against him being involved. She simply is beginning to wonder if Javier is looking at too large of a crowd to pinpoint the killer.

"Peter, can I ask you a question? And, if you do not want to answer it, simply tell me so. I will not be offended."

"What is your question, princess?"

"Obviously, Nicholas is involved with a lot of good things. Do not take this the wrong way, but is he hands on with every little project? Does he not trust a team of professionals to handle the overseeing for him?"

Peter gives a tight smile and replies, "To state this simply, NO! Mind you, our lives are a bit more complicated than his because we work to pay bills and take care of ourselves. Nicholas simply decides how to spend his money and inspire other people to spend their money the same way. So, with lack of tasks and this very large house, I am sure he takes on more than actually needed to simply battle boredom."

Angela laughs and tries not to choke on the food in her mouth. She imagines Peter states it perfectly. She spends most of her week cutting up dead bodies to define why they died. Peter creates meals and keeps the kitchen in order. Everyone has tasks to do during the week to distract their attention. Yet, Nicholas really does not need to do so. He simply wants to do something.

"I simply wondered." states Angela.

"Now, let me ask you something."

With her mouth full, Angela simply nods in agreement.

"Did you tell Nicholas to grow the beard perched on his face?" asks Peter.

Angela's eyes widen as she takes a drink to wash down her food. She was surprised to see the hair growth on Nicholas's face when he greeted her last night. She did not mind seeing him with a beard. Simply, just unexpected.

"No, I did not tell him to grow a beard. We had not seen each other for a few days. I was surprised seeing it last night. Do you not like it?"

She watches Peter shake his head in disagreement while he toys with a dish towel. He apparently has a bit to state about it.

"Princess, he is simply attempting to hide a stupid mistake. Please tell him to shave it off because he will not listen to me."

"Mistake? What mistake causes you to grow a beard?" asks Angela.

As Peter begins cleaning up his kitchen, he replies, "On one of those evenings you were away, he apparently drank himself into a stupor, fell and managed to smash his glass, which sent pieces flying through the air that cut his face. He will not admit it, but he simply desired to hide the little cuts on his face."

Angela finds the scenario a bit odd. She hates to think Nicholas drank himself stupid because she was too busy with Addison. And, even if it is how all of it happened, why not leave the marks alone and demand special treatment when she returned. Most guys would handle it that way. Of course, Nicholas is not like most guys.

"Wow, I shall do so." states Angela. "Peter, who does Nicholas spend time with other than me? I hate to think he was here alone drinking in abundance."

Peter shuts the dishwasher and releases a deep sigh. Angela watches him turn around slowly with a look of concern on his face.

"Nicholas, does not have friendships. The companies he hired to clean and landscape were hired through me. I simply knew the owners from spending time with them. He hired me through a single ad of a private culinary competition."

Angela is a bit shocked. Their interactions with one another caused her to believe Nicholas was friendlier with those working for him.

"Did you simply get closer after he hired you? A bit odd to place all the decisions of home upkeep to one person, but not entrust people with other projects."

"I honestly believe he gave me the authority because he simply knows nothing about running a house this size."

Angela laughs as she takes a sip of her Coke. She imagines the upkeep of such a large place is unusual for a great many people. She knows she would need to learn a bit to coordinate everything properly.

"So chances are Nicholas was drinking alone when all this happened?" asks Angela.

"Neither you nor I were here, which means no one was with him."

Well, she can be a bit thankful for that. She does not desire any competition.

"So we are the only ones who actually see him on a personal level? The housekeepers or gardeners do not have close association?"

Looking a bit annoyed, Peter replies, "No, princess, they do not. They complete their work during the day, which is usually when Nicholas is gone. If he is not in some crazy meeting, he is at the house in the wooded area."

House in wooded area? Angela does not recall anyone mentioning another house. With his home being so large, why would he need another?

"I do not believe I ever heard of this other house. Where is it? What does Nicholas do there?"

Peter takes a seat on one of the stools and replies, "At the back of the house, you probably noticed all the trees creating the look of a forest. The house is located back there. Exactly what he does there, I am not sure. When I began working here, he told me he uses it as his work place. He said it helps him mentally to have a location other than his home to do his work, which I can understand a bit."

Angela nods in agreement. Keeping work from home is one of the family rules. Her heart skips a few beats as she thinks of Nicholas speaking with her father. She is not ready for them meeting yet, even though they seem to think the same. Well, probably on just that one thing.

"As for talking with housekeepers or landscapers, I can tell you it is best to just not do so. Do not get me wrong about associating with the masses because it is something I do a lot of and very well. However, some ex-convicts are best to speak only with ex-convicts. Nicholas does not have the proper social skills to see their point of view and understand their motivation."

As Angela watches Peter rise off his seat and begin looking in the refrigerator, she wonders if she should even mention Javier's request to speak with him. From what Peter states, she highly doubts he can provide much information. Yes, he may know the names of those working for Nicholas, but how would any of them get inspiration from Nicholas if they do not associate with Nicholas. She is a bit uncomfortable about dragging people into the mess Javier is sifting through and in no way wants to offend anyone. She will just keep her mouth shut for now. Perhaps a longer, in depth discussion with Javier will assist her more on properly handling the issue.

Chapter 39

JAVIER LOOKS OVER A map attached to the wall and attempts to figure out a pattern with the pins stuck in locations of bodies found. The murders happened in neighborhoods throughout the city. Unlike gang activity, one zone does not include all the crimes, which means the killer travels throughout the city, which is a bit unusual. And even more unusual is the fact all the victims committed a sexual crime.

He use to believe the killer desired to protect children. Then, the victim's crimes began to broaden. They were all still of a sexual element, but no longer just crimes against kids. Steve thought the dog one was truly a different killer. However, all the evidence and system of killing to display the body points to the same killer. Apparently, the killer finds sex with animals offensive as well. As do most people...

Javier hears the door to the room open and close. He is not sure who came in, but he doubts it is Steve since their argument an hour ago became a bit personal. He takes a deep breath and turns around to see one of the FBI agents take a seat next to his desk.

A bit odd decision on choice of seat. Javier wonders if the agent desires something or if Steve put him up to something. Steve always has trouble letting arguments die.

"Can I help you with something?" asks Javier.

"Nah, simply taking a break from reviewing the autopsies. Figured a little conversation with you will do me some good to get the images out of my head. I was never a fan of seeing dead bodies."

Javier nods and walks back to his desk to sit down. He imagines this guy sees a lot of dead bodies and they are more horrible than this case.

"Keep in mind, the pictures are always better than in person." states Javier.

The agent chuckles and asks, "Are you thinking of ideas on the killer?"

Javier is a bit uncomfortable sharing his thoughts about the killer with this man. Either the agent will agree with him or claim he is completely ignorant. They each are making their own case against the killer to see who is able to achieve more time for the killer once caught. Federal laws tend to give more time than state.

"I was attempting to figure out what job or lifestyle enables a murderer to feel comfortable in all the neighborhoods in town. The killer seems to be all over town."

The agent shakes his head and states, "You are looking at it a bit wrong. The killer is not killing in places of comfort. The killer is killing those they are comfortable killing, which is why the locations are all over town. Each victim has caught the killer's attention, which causes the killer to kill. The location of the kill and placement of the body means little to this guy in comparison to who the killer is killing. If caught in the middle of a kill, the murderer will probably beg to finish the job."

Javier's jaw drops. Perhaps, he can learn a bit more from this agent.

"Why is the killer so comfortable with the victims? Are you saying the killer is uncomfortable with a personal sexual desire and kills others rather than himself? Or, this is a teaching the victims to take their own medicine?"

"No, the killer is dissatisfied with the victims' crimes. The killer is probably a victim of a sexual crime of some sort. Our killer wants their crimes to end and places them on display for all to see. Our killer probably never saw justice for the crimes committed against themselves."

"I will say you are correct on defining motivation. Perhaps, I should look through past sexual victims' cases." states Javier.

The agent shrugs and replies, "One of our agents is speaking with those in charge of monitoring sex offenders to see if any of the victims hold a deep grudge. I doubt anything will actually develop in it though."

"Oh yeah, why not?" asks Javier.

"Well, once a sexual crime is committed, the attention always focuses on the person who committed the crime, which makes sense because society does not want it to happen to anyone else and wishes the victim privacy. However, sexual crimes tend to bury deep emotions in a person's brain. Even with therapy, those scars remain and constantly appear throughout their life. Unfortunately, the victim is left alone to deal with it and is forced to either tell people what troubles them or keep it all buried within. The criminal is eventually released from prison, but their victim is in a different type of cell for their entire life."

"Then won't your agent be able to look into victims and find the ones that need help?"

The agent chuckles and replies, "No, the victims are not kept track of after the conviction is over. It is up to them to seek help, which a good amount of them do. However, they are free to do as they desire. And, if the victim never told anyone about what happened, then there is no way of us knowing about it. Unfortunately, sexual assaults are the largest crime never reported."

Javier feels as if every hope he had of finding this killer just washed away. He cannot even fathom the amount of local sexual assaults not reported. Hell, until the recent murder, he did not realize sex trafficking was a big local business. These are the things people seem to ignore. Yet, the killer is not ignoring it and wants other people to pay attention, which makes it a bit harder to chase after the killer. Who wants to track down a killer who is doing society a favor?

"Say our killer is a former victim, how do you think the killer finds their victims? It is not like these criminals are advertising their business." asks Javier.

The agent takes out a stick of gum and begins chewing it.

"Your question is the hardest one to answer. The killer's victims derive from various walks of life, commit different sexual crimes and are of various ethnicity. Either the killer is viewing the crimes first hand without people realizing it or a vigilante squad is telling the killer about the crimes."

Makes sense to Javier. Though he does wonder if the killer's victims are accidentally showing the killer what they do. Where does he see it?

Obviously, the human trafficking is easier to recognize, but what about the others. Is it possible the killer is a psychologist treating the victims' victims? Or perhaps someone who works in the office of a psychologist? This will allow sight of the victims and possible access to the medical records.

Javier is not sure how to think right now. Perhaps, the chef Angela was going to speak to knows a bit more. Something deep within him knows Nicholas Payne is somehow connected to all of this. He is not sure how, but he knows there is a connection.

Chapter 40

ANGELA LOOKS AT THE menu as kids go running past her booth. She did not expect an evening at a pizza place with Nicholas. Yet, she will still enjoy being here with him.

His arrival home was a wonderful moment. She was reading a book in the bedroom when he came home with a large box of chocolates for her. Though, she was not permitted to eat any of them yet. She imagines if she had argued the decree, Nicholas would have surrendered, but the moment simply led to love making. She is not sure if she should think of it as love making. However, it seemed much more intimate than sex. She felt as if something internally was passed between them. Whatever it was, it was more than sex.

"Do you have a preference on what we order? I eat about any kind of pizza." says Nicholas.

"No, the only thing I cannot stand is anchovies." replies Angela as a toddler stands up in the booth behind her.

"Sit down!" yells an angry father.

Angela's eyes widen at the evil tone of the father's voice. She wonders if the man simply had a bad day or is always like that. At the moment, neither really matters because her only concern right now is Nicholas and their time together.

She looks up from the menu at Nicholas and realizes he is sending a threatening stare to the father behind her. Well, it looks threatening to her.

"Is everything okay?"

Nicholas looks to her and the threatening look diminishes. Yes, she was right. And the thought of a strong man standing up for a toddler against an evil father makes her want to do so much with him. Obviously a huge sexual fantasy, but she likes the fact he stood up for a small child with a simple stare.

Angela hears the toddler laugh as the child leans over the back of the booth and smiles at Nicholas. He smiles back and Angela's heart completely melts. They have not discussed anything about the future. Yet, she is understanding his love for children, which is a plus for a man when marriage may develop. What is she thinking? She needs to calm her imagination down a bit. Marriage is far away since they really have not even spoke about a relationship yet.

"That is it! Restroom time!" yells the father as he stands up and yanks the toddler off of the seat.

"Like hell you will!" yells Nicholas as he rises.

The child begins to cry as the father turns around and asks, "What? How is this any of your concern?"

Angela watches an anger come over Nicholas she has never seen with anyone. As his fists begin to clench, his body becomes stiff as an evil glare casts towards the father. She wonders if the toddler is crying from the father's threat or if Nicholas scared the child.

"Nicholas, lets just simply order. I am sure the gentleman simply wants to talk to his child in a stern voice."

Angela is not sure what the man's intentions were, but she at least supplies a moment for him to think about his intentions. The child was not really doing anything horrible. She understands the man wanting the child to sit properly, but a toddler does not always comply.

Nicholas looks to Angela and takes a seat as he watches the man and toddler walk to the restroom.

"I am sorry. I let the moment get the best of me. I simply hate people beating on their kids."

"I understand completely. My parents spanked me as a small child, but it was nothing harsh. Then, when I could comprehend cause and affect more, they found other ways to punish me."

Nicholas smiles and looks to the menu again. As the waiter walks up to the table, a loud scream from the toddler is heard. Before Angela can say anything, Nicholas rises out of the booth and runs towards the restroom.

Unsure of what shall happen, Angela chases after him. He reaches the bathroom door and slams it open. Shocked by the loud noise, the man stops from striking the child's behind and looks to see who entered. His jaw drops when he sees Nicholas in the doorway.

Angela watches as Nicholas looks to the toddler and sees the child's tears streaming down its face as the father tightly grips the child's wrist. Angela is shocked to see how red the child's wrist is and worries the child's behind is even redder. Before she can say a word, Nicholas marches across the room and plants a right jab in the man's face.

The man falls to the ground as blood begins to gush out of his nose. Hanging on to the child's wrist, the man pulls the child down with him. Nicholas sees the crying child falling and moves quickly to keep the child from hitting the floor.

"You fucking monster. What are you doing? Let go of my kid. Someone call the cops!"

As Nicholas stands the toddler up appropriately, he replies, "Yes, someone please call the cops. Overbearing prick! Keep your hands off your kid."

Before the man can reply, Nicholas turns around and takes Angela's hand.

"Shall we go sit down?"

Angela is unsure of a proper answer. She wants nothing more than to return to the table and jump back into the moment they were once having. However, she is sure the police will arrive soon as she sees their waiter on the phone. The childish thing is to run and hope no one knows who you actually are when the police ask. As an adult, she knows they should wait for the police.

"What have you done to my husband, you bastard?" yells a woman as she runs towards Nicholas.

Nicholas drops Angela's hand as he turns towards the woman and yells, "Taught him the pain and fear he is inflicting on your child. Do not tell me you support that abuse!"

The woman quickly punches Nicholas in the face. Angela does not believe it affected him as she watches Nicholas push her back from him. The woman looses her balance and falls to the floor.

The police rush into the restaurant as the waiter points towards Nicholas. Angela watches Nicholas place his hands in the air without warning from the police. As he waits for them to reach him, he looks to her and states, "I am sorry, baby. Why do you not take my keys and wallet? I am sure they will let you order something to go. Just head to my house and I will see you sometime tomorrow."

As the police begin placing Nicholas in handcuffs, Angela attempts to understand all that happened. Is this a dream? A nightmare of some sort? How does a man fall into such an emotional rage over a child he does not even know?

Chapter 41

ON A DULL DREARY MORNING, Javier enters the police station and sees the usual unemotional faces he sees every Monday through Friday. Thankfully, he rarely sees any of them on the weekend. And, if he does, it is usually at a kids' soccer or baseball game. Since he coaches teams in his spare time, he cannot really get out of seeing them then.

He turns down the hallway leading to his office area. As he progresses down the hallway, Steve jumps out of a room and races towards him. He gets a little excited because Steve never greets him this way. Something must have happened.

"You are not going to believe who the police picked up last night. It is unbelievable." says Steve once he reaches Javier.

"Okay, who did they get and what are the charges?"

"Lets get into the office. This conversation will lead to things I do not want others to hear."

Javier nods as they begin walking to the office. He hates to admit it, but Steve has built up his excitement. And, he did it without really telling him anything.

They enter the room and Steve shuts the door. As Javier takes a seat at his desk, he asks, "Okay, what is all this excitement?"

Steve drops himself into the chair next to Javier's desk and replies, "Last night, there was an assault at Tony O's pizza. Apparently, a man chose to discipline his toddler harshly for not sitting properly in the booth. The man at the next table first warned the man against doing it, but when cries were heard coming from the bathroom, he rushed into the bathroom and assaulted the father."

Javier really does not know why Steve finds this so exciting. Perhaps he needs to jump out of detective work and just be a patrolman.

"Steve, why does this matter to us?"

Steve laughs and replies, "I knew you would just want to blow it off as if it is nothing."

"Then, what is it?"

"The officers arrested Nicholas Payne for assault and the father for child abuse. The man apparently used excessive force. Oh, the man's wife was also arrested for assault. Apparently, she punched Mr. Payne after he exited the bathroom. The kids were released to their grandparents."

Javier feels his body tense up. He understands why Nicholas lost his temper. Hell, he may have done the same thing. However, this definitely may provide an opportunity for them to get the man to talk to them.

"Is he still in holding? Or, did they release him?" asks Javier.

"No, he is still in holding. His lawyer is at the courthouse attempting to set up a bail agreement."

"Then we need to act fast before the lawyer succeeds because we know the man does not lack the money to pay for bail."

Javier stands up quickly and starts to head for the door. Before he opens the door, Steve states, "No need to rush yourself."

Javier stands still and looks at the door. He really wishes to beam Steve in the back of the head with something, but knows it will get him no where. Why does the man not simply state all the details at once? Is it a lack of communication training?

Javier turns around and asks, "What else have you not told me?"

"The FBI has also filed papers on the case. They are requesting Nicholas Payne be denied bail because he is a flight risk."

Javier slowly walks back to his desk and sits down. He understands their desire to keep him near. If Nicholas Payne leaves, either the serial killer will stop killing or kill even more. Either way, it is not good because even if the killings end, they still need to find the killer.

"Do you find it a bit odd they assume he will flee?" asks Javier.

"With the rich, it seems to be a common thing to do."

Javier nods and asks, "Who was with Nicholas Payne at the pizza place? I doubt he just randomly decided to pick up a pizza on his way home."

Steve begins tapping his palm on Javier's desk. He hates it when he does that.

"Mr. Payne was at Tony O's with the beautiful Angela Summers. They had not even ordered their food when all this began."

Javier doubts this could get any more stranger. Thankfully, Angela is smart enough to not get involved with it all. Though he does not completely understand why Nicholas lost his control so easily. He deals with ex-convicts, emancipated children and many other social misfits unable to hold their tongue and communicate in a violence free manner. Why did he lose control this time?

"Steve, did the FBI speak to you about Nicholas Payne in any way?"

Steve shakes his head and replies, "No. Why?"

Javier points to the board showing location of all the bodies and states, "I talked to one of the agents about the locations of all the victims. He told me I was looking at it the wrong way. I was looking at it as the killer is killing in places they are comfortable. The agent said the killer is comfortable killing who he is killing and the locations mean nothing. After I thought about it, I think he is right. What if our killer has a closer link to Nicholas Payne than we thought? What if it is Nicholas Payne?"

Steve stops tapping on the desk as he looks at the map. Javier knows he is thinking hard about what he just said and awaits an argument from him. However, Javier was comfortable stating it and he is willing to examine the possibility.

"I am not stating you are wrong, Javier. Not necessarily right either, but I see your logic."

The phone rings and Steve answers it.

"Okay, where this time?" asks Steve as Javier watches him.

Steve hangs up the phone and stands up.

"We need to get to the east side. Another body was found and they say it was done by the killer."

Javier nods and asks, "What motive this time?"

"This is an odd killing. The victim is in a private home. The killer did not pose him nor provide an obvious motive for punishment. Simply left a note and a collection of movies. Oh, and apparently, the victim has been dead for days. So, this is not going to be a pleasant smell."

As they walk out of the room, Javier wonders what is in the movies the killer wants them to see. He wonders if the victim is the one that made the killer a victim like the FBI agent stated. Why does this one victim get to stay in their home and wait for someone to discover the body?

Perhaps, this is the one they need to solve all the others. He is not sure whether to be happy or sad about finding the killer yet. Happy someone is not out their killing others, but if the killing ends, will the amount of sexual crimes increase? What if this person helps impede the growth of sexual assault? He hates to think of taking down something bad and enabling another bad thing as a service to society and the law. One victim is not better than another. And both crimes kill the person enduring it. The sexual assault victim may still breathe and go about life, but generally something inside of them died. And knowing that makes him want to kill someone as well.

Chapter 42

ANGELA SLOWLY TAKES a seat at the lunch table with Winston. She has been nervous about this moment since the night of Nicholas's arrest. How do you tell a friend about a romantic surprise and a nightmare at the same time when both things involve the same person?

She does not desire to appear as if she is covering up what happened by stating the arrest first to end with a happy story. Nor does she want Winston to believe she is involved with a psychotic man when stating it in order of how it happened. He is not psychotic. He simply lost control. At least, she thinks he lost control...

"How did your weekend go? Is Addison doing better?" asks Winston.

Thank the Lord, she is bringing up a conversation other than Nicholas. There is a lot she can state about Addie without getting into a horrendous debate.

"Yes, it felt as if he was kicking me out of his apartment the last day I was there. I knew it would not take him long to bounce back from what happened."

Angela smiles and takes a bite of her salad. She imagines the next question will be about Addie's injuries or about the police finding the attackers. Those are questions she will happily answer.

"Kick you out? When was the last night you stayed?"

Angela feels like screaming. She knows if she tells her when she left, then the events will be in order, which leaves her with a lot of explaining. She simply is not prepared to explain what happened at the pizza place because she is not exactly sure why it happened the way it did.

Angela takes a drink and replies, "I left on Friday evening."

She feels safe with that answer. She is not lying nor offering introduction to the surprise Nicholas sent. She simply stated when she left.

"Hello, ladies. Mind if I sit with you and eat?"

Angela quickly looks to her right and sees Javier with a Burger King meal in his hands. Amen, he is the person she needs to avoid further conversation about the weekend.

"No, please take a seat." replies Angela with a smile.

She watches him as he maneuvers past Winston and sits down next to her. She cannot help to notice his fragrant cologne and wonderful style of attire. He is a rather attractive man. Perhaps, Winston and him will hook up after this serial killer is caught.

As Javier unloads the Burger King bag holding his meal, he asks, "Angela, this is an odd question. Do you share the serial killer case information with Nicholas Payne?"

Angela refrains biting the piece of salad she was attempting to eat as Winston looks to her with an expression of uncertainty. She is sure Winston is confused because it is a rather odd question. She sits her fork down and replies, "No, I do not share information with him about my work. Is this concerning what happened Saturday evening? I am sure you heard about the arrest and my being there."

"Whoa, are you telling me Nicholas Payne was arrested? And you were there?" exclaims Winston.

Javier shakes his head and replies, "Angela, I am simply asking in case the FBI questions me. I doubted you would share any details. Out of respect for Nicholas, I simply felt it more polite to speak with you rather than bust into a room and attempt to intimidate him for an answer."

Angela nods and takes a bite of her salad.

"What was this arrest about?" asks Winston.

Angela simply looks down at her salad. Hopefully, Javier will understand and take over the conversation. Angela knows she lost control of this conversation before it ever really began.

"Mr. Payne became infuriated with a gentleman's aggressive punishment of a toddler and took matters into his own hands." responds Javier.

Angela cannot help smiling at his answer. She is not sure how he thought to describe it so, but it does cover the whole scenario without giving the bad details. She wonders if he thinks like that because he is a detective or because he was not there during the incident.

"Wow, good for him." replies Winston.

After taking a drink, Javier inquires, "Were you able to speak with the chef, Peter?"

Angela smiles and replies, "Yes, I did. I am glad you asked because I still need to ask him about what you requested. My conversation with him seemed as if he really has nothing to tell you."

Javier nods and replies, "Very possible he does not have the information we desire. What was your conversation about?"

"We talked about the people who worked at the house. Peter is the one who hired the companies to clean and landscape. Nicholas does not really have any contact with anyone at the house other than Peter and I. However, even Nicholas's time within the house is limited for he actually does all his work at a home located in the wooded area of his property."

Javier stares at her for a minute and then calmly asks, "Did you say there is another home on that property?"

Angela nods and replies, "Yes, according to Peter. He said Nicholas likes to separate work environment from the home, which I can completely understand. Staying inside the home all the time is probably boring as well as omitting a feeling of entrapment."

"What work does he do there?"

"I am not sure. I imagine it has something to do with his organizations."

Javier nods in agreement.

"Angela, do not bother asking Peter anything else. I do not think he knows anything."

Angela smiles as she takes a drink. She is glad that assignment is over. Now, she simply needs to talk with Nicholas to discuss what she adores about him and what she will not tolerate.

Javier begins throwing his lunch back in its bag and replies, "Ladies, I must get going. I just seen Steve pass by the door and I know he is searching for me. FYI, we traveled in with the latest kill and it is a bit rough to handle, which is why Steve did not join us for lunch."

As Winston and Angela laugh, Javier jumps up and tosses his lunch in the nearest trashcan. He rushes out of the lunchroom as they watch.

"Were you going to tell me about this Nicholas thing?" questions Winston.

"I was going to get to it. I simply wanted to tell you about some more positive things he did rather than getting arrested."

Winston shrugs and replies, "He saved a toddler from an abusive asshole. I say he did the right thing."

Rather than reply, Angela shoves salad in her mouth. She understands why Winston agrees with what he did. Angela imagines looking at the whole scenario as it was presented to her, it is very hard to disagree with what happened. However, there was much more to the whole incident. The child was still injured even though Nicholas stepped in. Everyone's evening dinner was disrupted. And, the other children of the couple, along with the abused child, were sent off to their grandparents as their parents were taken to jail. Stating the one action really does not cover the whole event. At least, not in her mind.

Chapter 43

NICHOLAS LOOKS AT THE small table in the tiny room as he waits for his lawyer. He begins pacing rather than take a seat. The room is larger than his cell. Yet, he still feels trapped and suffocated every moment he breathes. The frustration of fighting for the simple privilege of bail was never imagined by him. Now it is his reality, the obstacle has his full attention. Yet, he cannot help thinking of Angela and how she is dealing with this issue as well.

On his departure from the restaurant, she seemed so lost and confused. He imagines she never thought of him acting in the way he did. However, there is still a lot they need to learn about one another. He just hopes he is able to get out of here and prove to her there is reason to learn more about one another.

The door to the hallway opens and his lawyer steps in. He motions for Nicholas to take a seat. As Nicholas sits and pulls his chair close to the table, he holds his breath. The look on Fred's face is not a positive one.

"We meet tomorrow morning with Judge Thomas to present our argument for bail. I simply wanted to review with you the possibilities we may agree to in order to get you out of here. How are you handling it?"

Nicholas shakes his head and replies, "I feel as if every wall is closing in on me. I have not talked to anyone outside of here. And all the inmates in here either tell me about all their problems constantly or treat me as if I am a plague to avoid."

"Well, hopefully, this shall be your last night in here. The whole bail denial is a publicity stunt by the FBI because they are still looking for the serial killer. They feel if they go hard on you, then people will think before they commit a crime. I hate to tell them, but you and what you did is the last thing anyone needs to worry about. I would have done the same as you if I had seen it." states Fred.

Nicholas looks to the other side of the room. The fact the FBI is looking at his case frustrates him beyond belief. Yes, he committed an assault in a public place, but the general police department handles cases such as this. Perhaps, after Addison's attack, they are looking into all assaults to catch hate crimes. Yet, he cannot help wondering how many abused child assaults they are looking into as well. Shouldn't those people be the first to look at for possible serial killers?

"Do you really feel you have argument to get me out of here?" asks Nicholas.

"Nicholas, do not stress about the matter. The judge has no reason to worry about your ability to honor a bail agreement. You can easily agree to relinquish your passport to ensure you will not leave the country. And if they worry about you leaving the state, I can always request they place an ankle monitor on you."

Nicholas feels as if Fred stabbed him in the heart. The thought of an ankle monitor shows how he will simply leave one jail for another. He just cannot live with it.

"Ankle monitor? I will not agree to an ankle monitor. No one has the right to watch my every move."

"Calm down, Nicholas. I merely told you in case it comes up tomorrow. If you do not want it, then we will simply wait for them to suggest it as we pray they do not. Besides, they will need to prove it is needed first."

Nicholas jumps out of his seat and yells, "I will not wear an ankle monitor!"

He begins pacing as he shakes his head in frustration. Why did he not simply take up the matter with that man on another day?

With one act of assisting a small child, he has disrupted everything in his life. He still feels the act was necessary though.

"Keep calm. I highly doubt the prosecution will ask for it and extremely doubt the judge will grant such a request. With all you do in the community and your lifestyle, there is little belief you shall run off to avoid prosecution. My bigger worry is those parents filing a civil suit against you. The woman cannot really do so, but her husband may possibly win a case."

Nicholas shrugs and takes a seat in his chair. He does not care about civil proceedings. He did not harm the man enough to grant him outrageous amounts. So, to him, a civil suit is money well spent to issue pain to an abuser.

"Have you heard from Angela? I have been afraid to call her collect. I do not know if she will accept the call. If she denies the call, I will probably begin crying."

As Nicholas buries his face in his hands, Fred replies, "I have not spoke with her. I will tomorrow if you are not able to obtain bail. Talking with Peter the day after this occurred, he stated Angela returned to your home that night. She may very well still be there."

Nicholas unburies his face and simply nods. If she went home, Peter and her probably chatted about what happened. Hopefully, he talked some sense into her about waiting for him to be released before demanding answers. He does not want her to see this as being the real him.

"I spoke with Peter about another issue I wish you had told me about asking him to do." states Fred.

With a mocking smile, Nicholas states, "I simply thought duck may taste a bit better at Thanksgiving. Everybody always has turkey."

Fred stares at Nicholas in disbelief. Perhaps, it is a bad time for stupid taunts. They both know the subject Fred is talking about. He only asked Peter to do one thing other than his job. Unfortunately,

Fred often feels he has better connections to handle it, but Nicholas does not agree.

"I simply want to help Angela find her brother. She loves him and wishes to know where he went." states Nicholas.

"Yes, well, I wish you had placed Peter in touch with me to make sure no legal issues arise in his pursuit. By the way, he did find out the boy was alive when he left the area."

Nicholas is in shock. Angela is going to go into cardiac arrest with joy.

"He left the area? Is he still alive?"

Fred nods and replies, "Peter does not know if he is still alive. In our discussion, he and I agreed to allow me to hire a private investigator to find him because leaving for another state makes it so Peter's resources know nothing."

Wow, he left the state. Nicholas wonders what he is running from. Is it possible he avoids Angela to keep her safe? Why else would he not contact her after she became an adult and lived away from their parents?

"Is finding him going to place Angela in danger? I do not want her to chase after him in love only to be hurt in some way."

Fred replies, "That is why I am hiring a private investigator. The investigator will find the man and investigate the life he is currently living to make sure contacting him is safe."

"Wonderful."

Nicholas is so excited to be able to tell Angela something positive after discussing this ordeal. He hates he is probably buying his way to forgiveness with it. Yet, the information is what she is after and he really does need her to forgive him. If he does it just this once, he can still respect himself. Maybe...

Chapter 44

WALKING INTO AN EMPTY board room and sitting down, Javier feels a need for a cigarette. He has not smoked since his teens and does not plan to take the habit up again, but the desire is creating havoc within him. He knows the desire is from stress. When his captain told them they were to meet with the FBI this morning, Javier felt as if an anvil dropped from the sky and landed on his chest. He does not know if Steve feels the same way, but the damn thing is a bit heavy to bear.

He watches the FBI agents enter the room and shut the door. They all take seats across from him and Steve. There are numerous chairs around the table. Yet, they sit across from them as if this is an interrogation.

"Afternoon gentleman, we wanted to discuss both investigations to see if either of them gained information the other investigation does not know about. Lord knows both investigations followed dead ends on information provided."

As the lead agent uncaps his pen, Javier nods and replies, "Yes, we have at times too. Will be great to hear of your findings, as well as introduce new possibilities."

Javier watches as a few of the agents look at him with hope and others as if he is a bother to the day. He is sure they are as frustrated with as many dead ends as him and Steve. And for some reason, he doubts they obtained information that has him thinking a different angle. They should be a bit more optimistic in him sharing something they may not know. After all, they are all working on finding the same killer.

"The autopsy of the latest victim released this morning. By drugs used to kill the man, it is safe to say our killer is responsible. Yet, the crime scene does bring on another issue." states the lead FBI agent.

Javier hates he failed to read the report yet. Thankfully, Steve read it, but that does not mean he will see it properly. Well, not in the same aspect as Javier...

Javier asks, "What is the crime scene issue? Was it contaminated with false evidence?"

The agent shakes his head and replies, "No, there is no evidence contamination. As you know, there were tons of video recordings hidden in the bookcase of the room the victim was located as well as some placed near the body. We are still reviewing them, but it looks as if our victim either purchased or filmed child pornography."

"Sick bastard." mumbles Steve and the majority of the room nods their head.

Javier states, "Ok, we know the reason the killer killed the man. What is the issue? We know why the killer killed all of his victims."

The agent takes a deep breath and replies, "Yes, however, this one is different than the others. We believe the killer may have killed the man that made the killer a victim."

Javier wonders how they came up with such a conclusion. If it is true, then finding the recordings is the break they need to find the killer.

"Why do you believe that?" asks Javier.

"The killer did unusual things with this kill. The crime scene is the victim's home unlike all the other victims, which signifies a familiarity because all other victims were met in public places. The other telltale sign is the fact this victim was not displayed in a manner for all to see like the other victims. The killer may simply know the victim well, but after finding what is on the recordings, we feel the killer wanted to prove himself different from the victim by not placing an undesired display. The killer always wants to show why the victim died. Yet, this victim was displayed to no one. The killer probably is still trapped in the logic of a sexually abused child and wants to hide what went on between them."

A tear runs down Javier's cheek. He hates to think how many kids this last victim injured. He hopes the FBI are wrong though. If this is why the killer is killing, Javier will find it harder to search for the killer. Murder is evil. Yet, what this killer has ended, makes Javier want to give the killer a reward, which he knows he cannot do.

"How far back in time do the recordings go?" asks Javier.

"As I said earlier, we are still reviewing them. I believe they will go pretty far back in time. Some of the discs seem to have been transferred from another device, such as VHS. The picture is too grainy to be anything recent."

Javier wonders how many child pornography victims there are in the region. Better question is how many child pornogrpahy victims will admit it when asked. He hates to think they shall victimize the victims again simply to catch a killer who is doing what most of the child victims probably dream of doing.

"Rather than us reviewing the recordings, can we simply get a report from you?" asks Javier. He knows he cannot stomache the autracity on those recordings.

"Yes, we can send you one. One of the hardest things for our agents to handle is recordings like these. Has anyone in your office found anything interesting we should know about?"

Javier looks to Steve and watches him shrug. As always, Steve leaves the vocalization of their thoughts to Javier. He will argue with Javier day and night about a case, but refuses to speak to anyone else.

Javier states, "There is someone I find interesting. I have yet to discuss it in great length with my partner though."

Steve slowly turns to him and glares. Javier simply continues to look forward. If Steve wants to leave the vocalization of the investigation to him, then he is going to present it how he wants and with what he thinks.

The FBI agent states, "We would love to hear it."

"I no longer believe the killer is attached to Nicholas Payne. With all the interviews I have done, it appears no one is really completely attached to anything he does. He really does not communicate with people other than his fund raising events."

The agent replies, "Very possible, but we still believe he is connected to the killer in some way. In our work, the psychotic does not generally live in the life of the one they worship. Often, the psychotic thrives on the publicity of the idol."

Javier wonders how much he should discuss with them. He learns a few things from them often, but he doubts he will convince them what he believes.

"Did your interviews with Nicholas Payne lead to anything? Why did you request denial of bail?" ask Javier.

A few of the agents chuckle as the lead agent replies, "He basically refused to speak with us without his lawyer, which lead no where. The bail denial was simply a play to get him to open up to us. Unfortunately, it failed and he was released on bail this morning."

Javier was not aware of his release. This changes his attitude a bit. He feels energized to find out more information since his target is roaming again. Javier wants to leave the room now. Once Steve and him are alone, they can plot an investigation to prove Javier right or wrong. Steve will want him to be wrong. However, Javier is confident more investigation into Nicholas Payne will lead to his arrest for these murders.

"Now, as I advised my agents, everyone needs to pay attention to arrests made around town. If the latest victim is responsible for the internal hurt of our serial killer, then the victim's death may cause something to go wrong with our killer's thinking, which may cause mistakes and lead us to them."

Javier jaw drops as he thinks of the arrest of Nicholas Payne. Does the lead agent not realize he simply described what possibly happened at the pizza place?

"How do you know it will not end the killing?" asks Steve.

"That may possibly happen or the killings may continue. If the killer's mind remains on stopping the sexual crimes, the killer will not stop due to boredom because we all know sexual crimes happen somewhere throughout the day. If the last killing helped the killer resolve an internal issue, then we will still investigate all we have until the killer is found."

Javier doubts the killer stopped. If he was the killer, he would not stop. You do not hold pain deep and allow it to drift away with one resolve. Especially, when the death of one person does not resolve the whole issue. If the killer was a victim of child pornography, then the pain has not ended for the videos likely are shared with others throughout the world. Those sick bastards stick together.

"I am going to throw this thought out there. I spoke with some people about Nicholas Payne. I believe he may actually be the killer. He has all the ability to do so. And, the pizza incident may be what you are telling us to look for in a lead."

Javier watches the agents as they think of what he stated. Thankfully, they do not appear as if he is a madman. They are not exactly looking as if he made a wonderful discovery either. They seem to simply think on it.

The lead detective replies, "We cannot investigate on assumption. Mr. Payne does have resources to hide such crimes. Yet, it does not mean he is the killer. The pizza place was simply a loss of anger. I suggest sticking to the evidence to find more leads."

Javier simply nods in agreement. He knows they do not desire to falsely accuse someone of murder. Of course, neither does he. The moment simply shows he has to convince Steve the route he wants to look is the proper route.

Chapter 45

AFTER A DAY OF NON-stopping questions from co-workers, Angela decides to spend the gloomy evening watching a movie with a large glass of wine. She really does not care which movie as long as there is no violence. With the incident on the weekend and the questions about the incident today, she is sick of the sight and discussion of pain. She simply wants to think happy moments.

As she picks up her remote, she hears a knock on her door. Imagining it is a neighbor, she simply walks to door with remote in one hand and wine glass in the other. She realizes one hand will need to be free in order to answer the door and sets her wine down on the kitchen island in passing. Without looking through the peephole, she opens the door and finds Nicholas looking into her eyes.

Angela feels a slight anxiety overtake her. She knows it is senseless since he will not hurt her. Well, she does not believe he will hurt her.

"Good evening, Angela. I was released today and feel you deserve an explanation as well as an apology. May I come in?" states Nicholas.

Angela opens the door a bit more as she nods in agreement. With the words "deserve an explanation as well as an apology", she mentally forgave him. She does not intend to tell him though.

She closes the door as he looks around the room. She imagines the place is a bit small to him. Oh well, not everyone is a millionaire. She simply wishes the place was a bit cleaner for his first visit to her place.

"Can I get you anything to drink? A glass of wine perhaps?" inquires Angela as she places the remote on the island and picks up her wine glass.

"No, I am fine. Thank you."

"Why do we not move the conversation to the living room then?" states Angela as she grasps his hand and begins walking out of the kitchen area.

She feels his hand tighten around hers as if he was a small child afraid of being separated from a parent. She assumes what happened made him think of losing her. Though, she will need to get an exact definition of what they are to one another and what better night to do it than tonight.

Angela leads him in front of the couch and places her wine on the living room table as they sit. Perhaps not having the wine in her hand will entice him to be more open since she will not have anything challenging her brain nor a glass weapon in her hand. Not that she intends to use the glass as a weapon...

"First, let me say I am sorry for losing my control during dinner the other night. I should have simply called the police on the man. I just cannot stand to hear a child in pain." states Nicholas with an intense, sorrowful expression.

Angela realizes he is emotionally hurting in some way. She is not sure how to reply without appearing heartless. She did not like him getting arrested, but it is not like she did not want the matter to end as quickly as he did.

"Nicholas, I understand why you did what you did. And the child is probably very thankful you did. I simply hated seeing you arrested." replies Angela.

She knows the emotion of the incident is a bit more than what she is stating. Yet, she does not know if she should ask why he did not think of her before rushing into a restroom. What if he states something she does not care to hear? What if he replies "because your a big girl, Angela" just like her brother use to do? The whole scenario of spending time with someone you love and then them disappearing is simply too familiar with her.

"Yes, I imagine the kids are in a better place than that night. However, I want us to be in a better place than that night as well. I do not want you angry at me and walking away from me as I did you that night. I should have stayed with you and tackled the matter together. If I had..."

Before Nicholas can finish his statement, Angela pushes him back with a fierce kiss. Her hands wrap around his neck as his wrap around her back. She simply heard enough from him and wants him to feel it internally.

She stops kissing and leans her forehead against his and states, "You are forgiven. Now, let us not allow it to happen again."

"I pray it never shall." states Nicholas as he leans back further and pulls her with him.

She rests her head near his shoulder as he begins running his hand up and down her back while resting his chin near the top of her head. Angela wishes the world to disappear and allow them this simple moment. No sadness, no death, no anger and no sorrow. She simply wants to relax with the man of her desire. Can she have just a brief moment of it without someone ripping it away?

"Angela, I have something else I need to tell you."

Angela hopes he simply wants to tell her something about how he cares about her. Or, he wants them to be in an actual relationship. She does not want to interrupt the moment with heartbreak.

"Okay." replies Angela as she rests her palm against his chest. She does not know what his intention is and it is beginning to scare her.

"I spoke with Peter. He found some information on your brother. My lawyer, Fred, is working on hiring a private detective to find out more because apparently your brother left the state."

Angela feels absolutely ignorant for thinking the matter he wanted to discuss was them. He simply wants her happy and is willing to go the extra mile to show it. She rises off his chest and asks, "You really found out about him? What did you hear?"

Angela watches a large smile cross his face as he runs his hand through her hair.

"Peter found someone who knew he left the area to live in another state with some girl. Apparently, they once were an item on the streets, but they took off for some reason to another state. No one heard anything about him after he left."

Angela is in shock he has not attempted to contact her. They are both adults now. Their parents no longer control either of them.

"I do not understand. Why would he not attempt to contact me after all these years if he is still alive? Not that I want him dead, but I have embedded in my head he is probably dead since I have not heard anything." states Angela.

Nicholas pulls her back down on his shoulder and states, "He simply may think you will tell your parents and he still does not want them to know. Or, and please forgive me for stating this, he may be dead. Peter only found out about his departure. Fred's investigator has the duty to find out if he is still alive and his current lifestyle."

Angela realizes Nicholas thought a little more about this matter than herself. However, her emotions are wrapped in it. Thinking clearly on the matter is not always the option with emotions involved.

"I only talk to my parents every now and then. Like most, I only see them around the holidays. So, I am positive I can keep him a secret." states Angela. "Though, what do you mean about current lifestyle?"

She feels Nicholas shrug his shoulders and then he replies, "People change throughout life. Your brother may lead a perfectly normal life with family. Or, life sometimes does go very negative and he may be a raging drug addict more willing to kill you for your money than talk to you."

Angela breaks into laughter. She understands Nicholas's concern, but if he wanted money, then he would have already contacted her.

"What??? It is possible. He may have had a brain injury in some way causing him to become a psychotic individual."

She looks up to Nicholas and replies, "Perhaps, he is our serial killer and is killing people because he cannot find access to his long lost sister. Your locating him can resolve the murders."

Nicholas simply looks into her eyes. After a few moments of silence, she begins to feel a bit odd. She is not sure he is taking the comment as she intended.

"You do realize I am joking?" asks Angela.

Nicholas smiles and replies, "Yes, I simply wonder how you came up with a crazier story of what your brother's possible life is like than I."

"One of my hidden talents."

Angela rises off his chest and straddles his lap as she wraps her arms around his neck. She looks into his eyes as his arms ascend her back and pull her closer. With the beginning of a kiss, she knows how this evening shall end. And, she has no intention of stopping any of it to talk.

Chapter 46

"NO, WINSTON, I HAVE not heard from her. I am sure she is perfectly fine. Her worshipping idol was released yesterday. I am sure you can figure out what took place." states Addison as he stirs his coffee.

The last thing he expected to wake up to was a phone call concerning Angela. The girl is low on his list of worry right now.

"Okay, Winston, I will let her know if I speak with her. Goodbye."

He hangs up the phone as he takes a sip of his coffee. Hopefully, he may now retreat to his veranda to read his magazine. The article displayed on the front seems very interesting.

As he takes a step forward, his door bell rings. He looks to the door and wonders if it is possible to ignore it. Doubtful since Winston is already searching for Angela. Angela is probably at his door right now. He never understood how women manage to lose one another, but crisscross one another repeatedly during the hunt for one another. If one will stay in place, then the search for one another is much simpler.

Without looking through the peep hole, he opens the door. He grips his coffee tighter once he sees Angela is not at his door. Instead, a man in a suit. He knows it is probably not someone to assault him because he doubts anyone will wear suit to do so. Yet, he has no idea why this strange man is ringing his door bell.

"Hello. I am Detective Steve Olsen. May I speak with you?" states Steve as he flashes his badge.

Addison is not sure why this is taking place. Yet, he is intrigued a bit. He knows it does not deal with the assault and cannot fathom another reason to talk to him.

"Yes, please come in."

The detective enters the apartment while slightly looking around. Addison motions for him to follow him and heads to the living room.

Once they are seated, Addison asks, "What do you want to know from me? I am a fountain of information, but often told what I know does not matter to anyone else."

The detective develops an odd expression and states, "I am simply looking for some information on some people you know. It is simply to develop an understanding of their mentalities."

Addison thinks he simply heard the oddest thing ever to come out of a detective's mouth. He is not asking about events happening. The detective wants him to assist in figuring out mental state of some people? Hell, if he knew how to do that, Addison is sure he would be a lot richer.

"I can try to assist you. Though I doubt I can offer much other than facts of things that happened. As a reporter, I tend to keep other people's emotions out of my head." replies Addison.

"One of the reasons I came to speak to you is your ability to leave emotion out. I am in an argument with my partner on something that could jeopardize an investigation as well as the department. I simply need some knowledge to convince him he is wrong."

Addison takes a sip of coffee and replies, "Okay. What do you need to know?"

"I simply need to know all you know about Nicholas Payne. I know you are good friends with Angela Summers and probably hear more about their relationship than any other person, which is one part of my interest. I also want to know if you know anything about his business dealings. Everyone we talk to either knows very little or nothing at all. Mr. Payne seems very reclusive to everyone with the exception of Angela."

Addison just lost a lot of interest in this discussion. What in all of Hades changed and caused everyone to contact him about Angela this morning? Maybe, he should go there to escape all this crazy mess.

"I am not sure I can offer you a lot of information either. All I know is the two have a love affair, aka sexual admiration, with one another. They do not spend every night together, but she is at his place often."

"Do you know anything about the other house on his property he works from?"

"There is another house on the grounds? Good Lord, how much room does one man need? Those two can have sex all over the property daily and I doubt they will cover it all in a year."

Viewing the detective's blank stare, Addison knows the man is not interested in hearing jokes.

Addison states, "There really is not much I can tell you. However, one thing I heard about Nicholas when he moved here is something you may find interesting."

"What did you hear?"

"Before one of his fundraising events, I set out to find out more about the man because no one knew anything. I was told by a rather sordid individual about Nicholas's childhood. He claimed Nicholas's parents used Nicholas as a child to make child pornography. He said it ended at some point and they moved away."

Addison watches the detective drop a few shades of color. He is sure it is the distasteful subject.

Steve asks, "Can I have the name of the individual you spoke with about the matter?"

"I can tell you. However, it will not do you much good because he was the victim with the dog. Had I known the man was into beastiality, I would have never spoken with him."

Addison watches the detectives jaw drop. He wonders if the man is ill with something.

"Are you feeling okay? You look a little ill?"

The detective stands and states, "I am fine. Thank you for asking. And, thank you even more for your time."

Addison stands and walks the detective to the door. As he opens the door, he shakes the man's hand and with a nod he is gone. Addison is so glad he never took up the crime beat when reporting. These detectives are too odd for him to talk with regularly.

Chapter 47

ANGELA PLACES HER purse into the locker and begins undressing to change into her scrubs. She was already informed of the lack of murder victims for today. Well, so far today, no murder victims appear. Hopefully, the maniac has taken a break from sending others to death. Lord knows there are millions of ways people find death themselves.

Completely changed and ready to work, she shuts her locker and turns the knob to lock it. She exits the room and heads towards the autopsy room. She simply hopes today's autopsy is interesting. She loves the challenge of finding out the why. When it is something simple, she is a bit disappointed.

As she is about to enter the room, she hears, "Angela, can I speak with you for a minute?"

She turns and sees Javier walking towards her. Perhaps, she is wrong about not having a murder victim today?

"I was about to begin an autopsy, but I can talk with you." replies Angela.

"Is there somewhere we can talk privatley?"

Angela is not sure why he will need privacy to tell her there is another victim. However, she does not always understand Javier's logic and then he generally displays it to her.

"We can talk in the autopsy room if you do not mind a dead body. The body is under a sheet because I have not begun my work." states Angela.

"Perfectly fine." Javier anxiously replies.

Once in the room, Angela begins pulling her hair back and working on disinfecting her hands. She may as well use the most of every minute.

"What would you like to talk about?" asks Angela as she soaps up.

"I need to ask you a bit more about Nicholas Payne. My partner told me some information causing me great concern about what you may know and not realize."

Angela desires to laugh. She cannot imagine anything she has not already told the detectives.

Angela replies, "I am not sure I can tell you anything else about my boyfriend. Other than he made a mistake one night at a pizza place, which I know you are aware of him doing."

As Angela dries her hands, Javier asks, "Are you guys an exclusive item now?"

Angela looks to Javier to see if he appears disappointed. Realizing his expression is completely the same as before she told him, she replies, "Yes, the other night he asked me to make our relationship a closer status."

"Okay, wonderful. However, I need to know a bit more on your relationship with him."

Angela cannot piece together why anything about their relationship is a concern for Javier. Unless, Javier is back to attempting to get a date.

"Javier, I do not believe my relationship is any of your concern when we only communicate for work."

"Angela, my concern has nothing to do with your relationship. I am following up on information I received that worries me as well as the FBI. I need to know about his psychological health. Can you simply answer my questions?"

The anger in his voice begins to make Angela a bit curious. Even in moments when he had a right to be angry with her, he never showed the kind of intensity he just did.

"What do you need to know?" asks Angela.

"Has Nicholas spoken with you about his childhood?"

"Actually, no, we talk about my childhood often, but he generally does not speak about his parents or his life as a child. I never press him on the matter."

With a deep exhale, Javier looks away. Angela worries he knows something she does not. And, anything involving Nicholas is her top concern right now.

"I must tell you something I have heard about Nicholas' childhood though. I did not hear it from him, but a friend whom heard it from someone else. My friend was told Nicholas' parents used him for child pornography and made money from it." states Angela.

Javier looks to her and nods as he replies, "Yes, we are hearing the same."

"Do you want me to ask him about it?" asks Angela.

"No, do not mention any of this conversation to him. We have found a large supply of child pornography with one of the victims. The FBI believes the same victim probably victimized our killer and our killer may be on the films we found. Unfortunately, if the story everyone is hearing about Nicholas' childhood is true, he may also be on those films."

Angela knows Javier is not stating all of what he wants to state. She is not stupid and knows what he is refusing to state about Nicholas.

"Do you believe it possible Nicholas is the serial killer?" asks Angela.

"There is a possibility. However, any of those children filmed may also be the killer. Or, the FBI may be completely wrong."

Angela looks to the floor as she wonders. She cannot absolutely clear Nicholas with an alibi since they have not been together on the night of the murders. And, not being together those nights, does not make him guilty since their relationship was only people spending time together whenever they chose to do so. Hell, some of the murders happened before she even met him.

'I am not sure how I can be of assistance. I cannot release nor convict Nicholas of presumed guilt. I am not a detective." states Angela.

"I understand you are not. I simply hope you can provide information on his childhood. Unfortunately, Nicholas Payne seems to keep it from everyone."

Angela smiles and states, "I do not tell a lot of people about mine either. I am curious about Nicholas' life. So, the conversation on childhood is easy for me to begin. If he tells me anything of importance, then I will let you know."

"Wonderful! Can I ask you one more thing?" replies Javier with a shocked expression.

"What?"

"Have you been to the house he works from? Or, do you even know what exactly he does there?"

Angela rolls her eyes and replies, "I found out about the house only a short while ago. No, I have not been in it nor do I know what exactly he does there. If my knowledge of the house changes, I will tell you."

"Thank you." replies Javier before he turns and walks out the door.

Angela shakes her head as she wonders what she just wrapped herself up in. Obviously, she has no issue finding out more about Nicholas and will not share anything harming him. Yet, if there is some connection with him and the murders, she is not going to hide his guilt either. Her main concern at the moment is finding out if he endured a childhood atrocity. Even if he is not the killer, battling victimization of child pornography can have harming affects. If she wants to continue being a part of his life and understand him as a person, then she needs to find out more. And, she will, but right now she needs to begin thinking about this autopsy and get to work. With a look to the ceiling and a prayer in her heart, she begins her work.

Chapter 48

NICHOLAS OPENS A FILE cabinet and looks through the folders. There are several things he needs to work on, but selecting the appropriate timing for each project is often the most complicated thing he faces in life. He simply wishes it was all done with a nod of the head.

Hearing the front door open and close, Nicholas slams the drawer shut. He wonders who has entered. No one has ever stepped into this house other than him. Well, as far as he knows, no one has.

"Hello? Do you need assistance with something?" yells Nicholas.

He is not sure if he should expect an answer back. If the person did not know he was here, they will not answer back because they are trespassing. Or, the person may want to speak with him, but is not familiar with his voice. He is not sure who would fall into that category. However, it could take place.

Wanting an answer in some way, he walks to the office door and opens it. No one is standing in the foyer, which makes him a bit more nervous.

"Hello? I heard the door. You need to make yourself known." shouts Nicholas.

With the continuing silence, Nicholas wonders if he should begin looking for a weapon. He slowly enters the foyer and is a bit shocked when Fred leaps out of another room.

"I am sorry, Nicholas. I need to speak with you on something and Peter told me you were here. I simply entered and became lost looking for you."

Nicholas takes a deep breath and replies, "Next time, simply call to let me know and I will meet you at home. I like to keep this a very private place."

"Understandable you desire to keep a private space when you are in everyone's eye. I do not mean to trespass on private spaces. What exactly do you do here?"

Nicholas grits his teeth while wondering how long this conversation will last. There are things here he does not want anyone to see. As a conversation progresses, people begin to think they earn a freedom to move around freely. He is not sure Fred will keep himself from wondering where he does not want him.

"Follow me into my office."

After entering back into the office, Nicholas motions for Fred to sit on the sectional sofa in the corner. Nicholas sits on the opposite end of the sofa and states, "I do several things here. I handle my projects here."

"Oh, kind of like a large office away from home I suppose. Why is there a faint smell of chemicals? It smells a bit like a dark room would smell."

"Because the dark room once located at home was moved here when I had the arcade built. In my free time, I sometimes take pictures and develop them here because I do not want the house to smell. Can you please state what it is you came to talk about?"

Nicholas knows he is sounding angry. However, he does not care about how he sounds right now. He simply wants to get Fred out of here and get back to work.

"Well, the FBI came to my office asking me about you. They simply have a few questions I cannot answer properly. There are questions I am sure you do not have issues answering though, unlike the "who works for you questions"."

Nicholas feels his heart stop for a moment. Why does the FBI ask anything about him? They asked him enough questions while in jail. He told then what he was willing to tell.

"What kind of questions? I told them everything I am willing to answer when they interrogated me while I was locked up. Are you not my lawyer? I feel as if my life is under attack and you are simply making friends with them." yells Nicholas.

"Nicholas, calm down. The absurdity of the questions asked is the only reason I am confronting you about it. I do not believe you have any information for them and am not willing to give it if you did unless you desire me to tell them. I simply believe answering a few ignorant questions will direct them somewhere else."

Nicholas stands and begins pacing. His heart is racing a mile a minute. He cannot understand why the FBI is so concerned about him. He doubts they even knew his name prior to his arrest. He knows Javier probably pushed them in his direction. He still attempts to get the beautiful Angela. Javier needs to look somewhere else because Angela is his.

"What questions do they want answered?" asks Nicholas.

Fred smiles and asks, "When you were a child, were your parents abusive? Did you have to do things you did not want to do?"

Nicholas shakes his head and replies as he continues to pace, "All children are forced to do things they do not want to do. I could call them abusive, but that is not necessarily correct. They never beat me, but punishment was always what I had to think about when deciding upon going against their wishes."

"Did they ever have you perform in child pornography? Please do not get angry. It is the final question and I doubt the answer will be yes."

Nicholas is not sure how he wants to answer the question.

"By child pornography, what are you considering? Parents often take pictures of their naked children. Some consider it nature and others pornographic."

As he continues to pace, Fred watches his every move as if he is an attraction at a zoo. Nicholas does not care what is running through the man's head. He simply wants this conversation to end.

"I believe they are meaning video footage of you playing with your genitals, another child's genitals or an adult's."

Nicholas stops pacing and stares at the wall. His mind is completely blank and a calmness rushes over him. He turns to Fred and replies, "No."

Fred smiles wide as he stands up. He tells Nicholas, "Well, I have all the answers I need. Hopefully, the FBI will begin examining evidence and find their killer rather than annoy you. Have a good day. I will see myself out so you can return to your work."

Nicholas smiles and nods as Fred leaves the room. He cannot believe how this day is going. He is going to have to call Angela and let her know he is not available tonight. The questions built an anger in him he does not want her to see. However, now is the perfect time to pick a project. A project that will release his anger and free someone from atrocity. He knows he needs it.

Chapter 49

THE TOPIC IS CROWDED tonight as Ian MacGregor takes a sip of coffee. The usual crowd of holier than though book analysts are seated in the best spots. The straglers hoping for a conversation fail to flock around them and Ian wants to laugh at their desperation. He is only there for the coffee. Well, and to cool off from dealing with annoying nieces and nephews.

He wants to move out of his sister's house, but the cost of housing sky rocketed. He works simply to make life more enjoyable. Paying someone to have a roof over your head that you will rarely be at is not enjoyable to him. Why should he pay for other people to enjoy their life?

He empties his cup and shoves it towards the back of the bar for the barista to collect. He wants out of here before tonights performance begins. He cannot believe the place actually pays some sap to speak in a rhythemic tone as the crowd pretends to really understand the meaning of what is said. Its all a waste of time and money if you ask him.

Exiting the building, he looks around to see if anything appears to be happening at any of the clubs in the neighborhood. With very few people going in and out of the buildings, he knows it is simply another boring night. He sometimes wishes to move away to a more exciting place, but this is the only place he knows. He has lived here all his life.

"Pardon me, can I get a ride from you? My friends and I got into an argument. Unfortunately, I rode with them and I do not want to wait for around for a ride home." asks a well-dressed gentleman.

Ian generally does not give rides to anyone. Yet, this guy seems trustworthy and suitable to be friends. Ian knows nothing about him, but his clothing says a lot.

"I am afraid it will have to cost you fifty dollars." replies Ian.

He is no fool and never works for free. If this guy had thought about himself rather than what his friends can do for him, then he would not be in the position he is in. And, best way to teach him is to charge him.

"I am more than willing to pay you. I live on Pemberton Circle."

Ian is a bit surprised on learning where he lives. Generally, only the financially endowed live there. Perhaps, this guy is someone he should want to know.

"My car is right there." states Ian as he points to it and unlocks the doors with a remote.

He watches the man enter his vehicle as he walks to the driver's side. He wonders why this guy is so docile. He was man enough to ask for a ride from a stranger, but then follows directions as if he is a child. Pointing to the car has him entering it and putting on his seat belt as if a parent instructed him.

Ian starts the car and pulls away. With the style of clothes and where he is driving the guy to, Ian feels its okay to collect the money at the end of the ride. Ian usually does not wait until the end, but something tells him this guy is okay.

After driving a few miles in silence, Ian turns on to Pemberton Circle. He loves the houses located on this road. They all have large yards and are often gated to keep everyone out.

"I am at the next house on your right side."

Ian looks at the house and asks, "How much did this mansion set you back?"

The man chuckles and replies, "I do not live in the house. I am employed here. My residence is a small house behind the mansion in a wooded area."

"Oh, is the house as nice as the mansion?"

"Yes. If you would like, I can show it to you."

"Alright."

Ian parks the car. As they exit the vehicle, Ian wonders what job this guy does and if they are looking for anymore people.

"Just follow me."

Ian follows the man. As they are walking, Ian wonders if he should collect the money now. He will hate having to bash this guys head in if he attempts to get out of paying him by showing him where he lives.

They begin walking down a stone path. Ian sees the houses chimney through the trees. He imagines this place is going to be beautiful and will strike a jealousy within him when he returns to his sister's and her bratty kids.

On the front porch, Ian sees the ornate Victorian knocker on the front door. He wonders if it is of any value. As he attempts to look at it closely, the man opens the front door without unlocking the door and walks in. Ian follows him inside as the man turns on a light and asks, "Do you not lock your door when away?"

"No, the neighborhood is very secure and all the cameras on the property record everyone coming and leaving the property."

Ian looks around the room and sees other rooms in every direction. He is very curious how the other rooms appear. The light does not shine into the other rooms, which has Ian even more curious for they look empty.

"Here is your money." states the man as he hands Ian a fifty dollar bill.

"Thank you." states Ian as he takes it from him and places it in his front pocket.

Ian thinks he needs to know this man a bit better. Not only did he not argue down the price of the ride, but he remembered to pay him without evening being asked. Apparently, this man has principals unlike most of society.

"Well, let me show you around a bit. Lets start in the basement. I have a private bar down there and I am sure you will appreciate it. And, while down there, perhaps we can grab a drink to take with us while I show you the rest."

Ian loves his hospitality. With a smile and a nod, Ian informs him he is ready to begin. The man turns to the left and fails to turns on lights as they walk through a room. He opens a door Ian assumed was a closet and flips a switch to illuminate the staircase. With the ability to see, Ian realizes the room they are in is empty. Oh well, the guy probably does not have use of the room.

He holds open the door and motions for Ian to enter. Ian descends the staircase The man is close behind him and states, "Once you are at the bottom, you will need to let me through so I can find the light. The one flaw the room design has is the location of the lightswitch. There are no windows in the basement and they placed the lightswitch on the other side of the room."

Ian chuckles as he reaches the bottom step. He quickly steps to the side to allow the man through. As Ian listens to his movement, he feels excitement build within. He wonders how the room will look once the light is on. He hears the man pick up something and wonders what it is he picked up.

"Did you find a bottle on the way across the room?" jokes Ian.

He waits to hear an answer, but hears complete silence. The man's movement is no longer heard. Ian wonders what has happened. Is it possible the room is much larger than he anticipated? Or, is the man actually a bit evil and intends to assault him to collect back the fifty dollars?

With each moment of silence, Ian feels a heavy burden of doubt. He wonders if he should leave.

"Hey, are you okay? Do you need help with something?" asks Ian.

Ian still hears nothing and decides to end the evening. He can return home with the fifty. He does not need to make a new friend. As his foot steps on the first step, something large descends on the back of his head. Ian falls onto the stairs and remains motionless.

Chapter 50

LAYING IN THE SUN WITH her eyes closed to battle the rays shining, Angela feels an arm across her abdomen and lips on her cheek. She smiles as the arm remains across her stomache.

"Nicholas, I realize you decided to turn over. However, if your arm remains across my abdomen then I will not tan properly. Your arm will leave an outline of where it was."

Nicholas laughs and replies, "Well, then everyone will know you are mine. I do not see it as a bad thing."

Angela simply smiles back and returns his arm to him. She imagined laying in the sun with him will cause problems. She was shocked when he asked her to do it. With all the skin cancer warnings, she has not layed in the sun since junior high school.

"Fine. I will need to find another route for all to know you are mine." states Nicholas.

As she turns on to her stomach, she states, "Well, I happily tell all I am yours. Letting others know will not be a daunting task with all the gossipers in town."

Nicholas makes a mocking cringe as Angela laughs. She wonders how many people actually do talk about them. Obviously, she is not the one sparking the gossip. All the busy bodies want to know who Nicholas is and what he does. And, all of that was before his arrest. Now, even more people are interested in him. An elderly lady stopped them the other day and congratulated him for protecting a young child. Before Angela could argue the proper way of calling the police, Nicholas simply thanked the woman and she walked away.

"Okay, lovebirds, I am keeping track of your time in the sun. You have gone too long without something to drink. So, I brought you these wonderful pink lemonade margaritas." states Peter as he lays the tray near their heads.

As he walks away, Angela shouts, "Thank you."

Nicholas hands her one of the margaritas. She takes a drink and wonders if life together will always be like this. Will they simply enjoy one another while others take care of the mundane tasks of cooking and cleaning?

"I have to commend, Peter. He does know how to make wonderful margaritas." states Nicholas.

Angela smiles at him as he rests his upper body on his elbows. Having rose to her knees to take her margarita, Angela sits cross legged and savors her drink. The day is going perfect, but she would love for a random pair of sunglasses to fall from the sky. She knows it will not happen. Instead of wishing, she looks down at Nicholas and admires his wonderful body.

"Tell me, Nicholas, did your parents ever do things you do not like?" asks Angela in attempt to keep a conversation going.

"Why do you ask about them?"

The sternness of his voice surprises her a bit. She was not attempting to unveil family secrets. However, she is truly interested in learning more about his childhood. She has already told him everything about hers.

"I simply want to know how your life was when you were a child."

"Life was fine growing up. We once had struggles, but grew past it."

"Oh, so like nearly every family in the world, money became a concern and they managed to move past it." states Angela.

In a near whisper, Nicholas states, "The troubles were not money related."

Angela is not sure she desires to hear what it was with the way he is communicating. Yet, she believes, the time is to let it all out now rather than another time. Why wait? The anger is obviously there and will remain until he realizes it is naught to her. Simply memories she wants to hear about.

"Then, what was it? Was drugs or alcohol the issue?" asks Angela.

"Look, I do not want to talk about them. They are dead. I live my life the way I want to now." yells Nicholas.

Angela is shocked such an angry tone came out of him. Apparently, he needs to deal with the emotions of his parents before he can share the memories. Angela simply looks at the blanket underneath them and drinks her margarita.

Nicholas sits up and looks to her as he states, "Angela, I am sorry. There is no reason I should be yelling at you because of them. I do have bad childhood memories, but usually keep them held inside. Perhaps, the sun is getting to me. I did not mean to yell."

Angela looks to him and replies, "It is okay to let the anger out now and then. Why do you not take me on a tour of where you do your work to get out of the sun?"

"I am not sure you really desire to see it since it really is nothing special. The house use to be the butler's home. Once he died, the previous owner decided to sell the entire property. I often wonder if he sold it out of heartbreak from his butler's death or if he was a complete prick that did not believe someone else could fill the position."

Angela laughs as she stands up and slips on her sandals. Nicholas watches her and asks, "You really want to see it?"

"Yes."

Nicholas stands up and slips on his flipflops. He, then, grabs her hand and begins leading her towards the stone path. She continues to look at the landscape as they continue down the path. In a matter of seconds, she sees the house. Nicholas is correct in stating the home is nothing special. With the mansion being so ornate, she expected the house to have a little character, but it seems almost like any house you see on any suburban street in America. Well, with the exception of the Victorian knocker. You generally do not see that on any suburban street in America.

Nicholas opens the front door. As they step inside, Angela asks, "Do you not lock the front door?"

"Why does everybody ask that question? I do not lock it. To get into the house, you have to walk past the mansion and security cameras are all over the property."

Angela nods and continues to look around. Nicholas was correct on saying it is nothing special. The rooms she can look into from the hall do not even have furniture. Of course, if he uses it as an office, then the rest of the house really does not need anything.

"Come this way and I will show you the room that actually has things in it." states Nicholas as he holds her hand.

Nicholas opens a door and motions for her to enter. Once in, Angela sees a desk in the middle of the room with a tall wooden filing cabinet off to the side. On the other side of the room is a sectional sofa. Yes, Nicholas is absolutely correct in stating this place is a bit boring.

As she is about to turn around and suggest they go up to the mansion, Nicholas's arms are around her from behind and he begins kissing on her neck. She wonders if he attempts to make the office a bit more interesting.

One of his arms slips away and he works on untying her bikini top. When the top drops to the floor, Nicholas' hand reaches down into the bottom of the bikini and begins massaging her clitorises. Angela gasps with pleasure as his other hand plays with her nipple.

He slowly moves her towards the desk. Once he reaches it, he takes his hands and places her hands on the top of the desk as he continues to kiss her neck. Within seconds, he drops her bikini bottom and his trunks. He enters her as he continues to play with her nipple and clitorises.

Angela is in complete bliss as her hands claw into the desk.

"Oh, my God, Nicholas!" cries Angela.

As the thrusting gets stronger, Angela continues to cry out. She feels her climax building, but does not want the moment to end.

"Tell me you want me forever." commands Nicholas as he pulls her head back by her hair.

Angela is turned on even more by his command and cries out, "I want you forever. I am yours."

Before he lets go of her hair, they both climax. Gasping for air, Nicholas slips out of her. They continue to stand as they were having sex. Nicholas begins to kiss her back. All Angela can think about is how special he made his office to her.

She turns around and begins kissing him softly on the lips with her arms wrapped around her neck. His arms wrap around her waist as she continues. She stops kissing and looks into his eyes as an odd sound occurs beneath them. She is not sure what it is, but it sounds like something is attempting to move and not succeeding.

"What is the noise I am hearing?" asks Angela.

Nicholas rolls his eyes and replies, "With the house located in the woods, wildlife attempts to make it there own. I have traps below. Either a rat or a raccoon managed to get stuck in it."

"Well, let's go down there and let it go."

Nicholas shakes his head and states, "No, I have people to do that. They take it to a nature reserve and release it. Don't worry about the poor thing. I leave food and water in the live trap to lure them in. I will call tomorrow and let them know they need to get it."

"Ok."

Angela just realized another caring factor about him. Most people simply place poison out and wish for the worst to happen to the animal. Nicholas simply works at getting the animal in a better place.

"Let's get dressed and head up to the mansion. I am a bit hungry now." suggests Nicholas with a wonderful smile.

Angela kisses him and begins looking for her clothes as she wonders if Peter has already made the meal. She is a bit hungry as well.

Chapter 52

ANGELA AND WINSTON enter into a store in hope of finding something to buy in the new arrivals. Angela really desires something to upgrade her style of dress. Nicholas owns so much she feels as if she needs to dress in designers when in public with him rather than whatever she likes. She really does not care what others think. She simply wants to show other women any play for him is going to be brutal and expensive.

"Hello, ladies."

Angela smiles as Steve steps to them. She is much happier when he appears than Javier. She gets along with Javier perfectly fine now, but there is no sexual undertones when talking with Steve.

"Hello." reply Angela and Winston.

Thinking of Javier, Angela remembers what he asked her to investigate. With Steve here, she can kill the task of tracking down Javier and supplying answers. Steve was not in the discussion. However, he is Javier's partner and working the same case.

"Can I give you some information to you to give to Javier? He asked me a couple of questions I did not have answers to, but now I do."

Steve looks a bit perplexed and asks, "Why was he asking you questions? Was it a personal matter?"

Angela wishes she had kept her mouth shut. Apparently, Steve is not in the loop of Javier's thinking. However, such operation between detectives will allow Steve to place Javier in check with his ignorant allegations against Nicholas.

"He came to my work about a week ago. He asked me about Nicholas's childhood and a building on his property in the wooded area." replies Angela.

"I think he simply wants to clear Nicholas Payne of any accusations before they get started. Mr. Payne is a guy people want to stick around."

Angela smiles and replies, "Yes, including I. I asked about his parents, but really only got emotion rather than answers. Apparently, his childhood was not the best and he refuses to talk about it."

"It happens very often unfortunately. He will let go of the pain eventually and talk about them. What about this building? I think it is the biggest thing in question because hardly anyone knows it is there and even less have actually seen it."

"Nicholas uses the building for working on his foundations. I recently saw it. The only room with anything in it is his office. The dark room attached to the office may have things in it, but I did not go in there. All the other rooms are empty."

Steve looks very surprised as he asks, "He has a dark room at the building?"

"Yes, he moved it from the mansion in order to build the game room. He says photographs are a small hobby for him when he is bored. He must not do it too often because I have yet to see a collection of photographs."

"Some people only photograph when they need to do so. Most photographers use digita now, but some still enjoy film developing." replies Steve.

By his expression, Angela believes he is thinking hard about something. Perhaps, he is piecing something together about the case. After all, she did an autopsy requiring her to remove nails and a lot of photographs.

"Yes, and Nicholas does not get bored too often with his organization and I. The latest thing keeping his attention is the wildlife attempting to live in the building. He sets live traps so a wildlife organization can release them somewhere else. However, the past few days, it seems the wildlife is stepping up their game."

"Oh, are they interrupting your time with Nicholas?" jokes Winston.

Angela laughs and replies, "Yes, they are interupting our time together. He places food and water in the live traps, but forgets to check them during the day. Twice now, I came over and had to wait for him to go the building to check them."

"He is leaving you to go check traps? Why does he not send his chef?" asks Steve.

"Peter is gone by the time he remembers."

"Well, I hope you ladies have a wonderful shopping experience. I need to look for my wife before she spends my entire paycheck buying things to get our kids to stop complaining about life."

Angela and Winston giggle as he walks away. Angela feels a bit of stress float away. Now, Javier has no reason to question her about Nicholas at work. If there was issues with what she stated, Steve would have shown more concern and asked more questions, right?

"What did you and Nicholas talk about in the office very few see? I am sure it was a very professional matter." states Winston with a gleam of laughter in her eyes.

Angela knows she is teasing, but she will be happy to tell her what took place.

"Are you sure you want to hear? It is a bit sultry as well as endearing."

The look of surprise washing over Winston's face leads Angela to believe she is very interested in what took place. She will play in a nice way and give just a few details.

"We went to the house so I could see what was in it. Showing me his office, sexual desire swept over him and together we satisfied the desire. However, during the process of gaining gratification, Nicholas demanded I tell him I want him forever and I happily stated it."

Winston simply nods and begins looking at clothes. Angela is a bit shocked at her response. She thought Winston would desire to know even more about what took place after telling her. Though there really is not anything else to tell about the moment. After it ended, they simply went to the mansion and finished up their day.

"I am surprised you are not asking more about him demanding forever." states Angela.

"Do not take offense, but it was in a sexual moment. He may have meant it deeply or it simply may have been a sexual domination thing."

Angela did not think of it as a domination moment. Nicholas usually is not dominant in sexual moments, but sexual moods can be odd and they were in his office.

"I did not think of it that way. I took it as a vow. Do you think I am wrong?" asks Angela.

"Angela, you were in the moment and know him better than anyone. I cannot tell you if you are right or wrong about the true meaning of what he demanded. Take it as it is. You do not define a relationship on one sexual moment. If we did, I doubt anyone would ever fall in love."

Angela giggles as they continue looking around at clothes. She knows the moment captured her heart. Thinking of it as a sexual dominance thing is not what she desires, but may be possibly what the moment was. She will simply need to spend more time with Nicholas and figure out the truth of the moment, which she planned to do anyways.

Chapter 53

JAVIER AND STEVE TAKE a seat in the conference room and wait for the FBI to begin their presentation of new evidence. Javier is feeling as if he lacks ability to find anything worthwhile lately. However, he does not have the same resources as the FBI. He simply has Steve.

The lead FBI agent stands after another closes the conference room door.

"I wanted everyone to meet and discuss new findings of evidence and possible leads. My video analysis team has reviewed the evidence found. The videos go from decades back to even present day. Whether the victim taped all of them or not, is yet to be determined. Child pornography is transmit throughout time. They trade the videos and images as most of us would trade baseball cards."

"Have you identified any of the victims?" asks Javier.

"We did identify a few from past convictions. The images managed to convict a few people, but the person filming the incidents was never identified. They run a tight operation where no one talks about one another. All the convictions were based on possession, not production."

Javier opens a folder he brought with him and hands a photo to the lead FBI agent. As the agent looks at the photo of a little boy, Javier asks, "Can you ask your video analysis team if they saw that child in any of the images?"

"Yes. Who is the child? Is the child involved in a criminal case?"

Javier takes a deep breathe because he knows an argument is about to begin. Even if the FBI buys into what he believes, Javier is positive Steve will argue against it. As he always does when Javier figures out something.

"The child is a grown man now. The photo you have in your hand is Nicholas Payne as a child. I have reason to believe I looked at his involvement completely wrong. I use to think the killer was motivated by him to kill. Now, I am leaning a bit more towards him being the actual killer."

The lead FBI agent passes the photo to another agent and asks, "Do you have any evidence leading to this assumption? We cannot simply pick out a person to accuse. Especially, when the person is well off and able to hire a great defense team that will also sue after false accusations."

Before Javier is able to answer, Steve states, "I have not spoken with Javier about possible evidence yet, but I have to say I agree with him. He asked Mr. Payne's girlfriend, Angela, a few questions. I saw her at the mall the other day and she gave me the answers."

Javier looks at Steve in shock. He cannot believe Steve is actually agreeing with him. What did Angela tell him.

The lead FBI agent asks, "What were the questions? And, how did she reply?"

"From what I gathered from her, Javier asked about Mr. Payne's childhood. Angela stated he blatantly refuses to talk about his parents and may hide some hate towards them. She does not know exactly what he hates about his childhood with them, but it does not seem to have been a pleasant experience."

Lead FBI agent replies, "I will have my team look at the photo to find out if his image was on any of the recordings, but do not get your hopes up because many a thing can cause childhood hate."

Javier feels a bit disappointed with the FBI, but is happy he will not argue with Steve about it anymore. He thinks the investigation just made a positive turn towards the possibility of solving the case.

"I want everyone to be aware about the possibility of the killer taking another route with the victim, which does cause us to wonder if the killer was not a victim of child pornography and is simply getting lazy with their work."

Javier finds the statement a bit odd. Everything he has learned about serial killers states they tend to follow a certain pattern in killing and only deviate from it when they are interrupted or victim has special meaning.

"I do not understand. What brought this thought on?" asks Javier.

"A recent report of a man who seems to have disappeared. His sister reported him missing a few days ago after speaking with her children when he did not return home. One of the kids admitted that he and his friends spread a rumor of sexual assault and abuse against his siblings in a hope the serial killer would target him. The kids apparently do not associate with their uncle well and did not believe false accussations would actually reach the killer. As we speak, officers are still searching for the man. This afternoon they are reviewing some security tapes from some businesses located around the coffee shop he was last seen."

"How does all that tie in with the killer possibly getting lazy in work?" asks Javier.

After a long pause, the agent replies, "It does not mean there is a change in anything. I am telling you all of this so you remember to keep your eyes open to everything. With gay bashiers and kids spreading rumors, we do not know if someone is attempting to act as the killer because they are against certain things. Just like we do not know the child pornographer actually knows the killer or if the killer simply decided he did not like his work."

By the negative tone, Javier knows he should have thought harder on what he was told. Rather than spark anymore anger, he simply nods and looks down at his note pad.

"Can I interject something I found out about recently?"

All heads turn towards Steve as the lead FBI agent replies, "Go ahead."

"Another question Javier asked Angela about was the other home on his property. Apparently, Mr. Payne does all his work there. Yet, people rarely visit the location and about all the rooms are empty except for his office and the dark room."

Javier's jaw drops as Steve continues, "She also stated the home is having a problem with wildlife breaking in. She said Mr. Payne is often returning there in the evening because he forgets to check the food and water left in the live traps. I asked her more about the dark room since most photographers use digital now. She stated it is a hobby of Mr. Payne, but she has not really seen any collection of photos. When building the arcade in the mansion, he moved all the dark room equipment to the house he works in."

The room is very quiet as all the agents think on what Steve stated. Javier thinks Steve managed to break this case wide open. He is not sure if he is happy or angry about it though. Yes, Steve is supplying information possibly pinpointing the serial killer, but all the answers are from questions Javier wanted answered after his suspicions began focusing on Nicholas Payne as the serial killer. Steve may not argue with him about it, but he is definitely stealing the thunder of solving it.

The lead FBI agent replies, "I am not saying with certainty you may be on to something with Mr. Payne. However, all you are stating paints a wonderful portrait of a place we need to look at very carefully. After my agents look at the security tapes this afternoon, I want to talk with you two about this a little further."

Steve and Javier nod in agreement. As Javier looks to Steve, he is unsure if he should yell at him now or later for stealing all the glory. The lead FBI agent continues on about other developments and Javier decides to take a rest for the moment. After all, if it leads to absolutely nothing, then Steve can take the blame for getting everyone's hopes up.

Chapter 54

NICHOLAS ENTERS HIS work home and heads towards the basement. With Angela entertaining Addison with a movie extravaganza tonight after an argument with his boyfriend, Nicholas hopes to find answers to the questions on his mind. Walking down the steps in the dark, he hears no sound. No movement, no sound of eating or drinking and not even breathe. He doubts what is in the trap escaped because he welded the cage himself. He reaches the floor of the basement and switches on the light.

Looking towards the cage to see if anything is dead, he views exactly what he expected to see. His prisoner looks back at him with hate while attempting to allow eyes adjust to the new light. Nicholas walks over to a stool and sits down.

"I see you are doing well within the cage. I know the food and drink could be a bit better, but I do not desire to entice you to stay." states Nicholas.

The man in restraint chains rises off the cot in the cage and walks to the steel bars. Nicholas hates seeing him in chains commonly used for inmates, but he does not desire to give the man free movement either. The removal of the mouth restraint was enough freedom after the man agreed to not yell nor argue.

"Let me out of here." states the man as he stands next to the steel bars.

"I told you what I need to end this. Confess to what you did to those kids and it will all be over." replies Nicholas.

"I did not do a damn thing to any kids!" yells the man.

Nicholas is in a internal struggle from Hell. He doubts this man tells the truth. He knows rumors do not always display the whole truth, but are generally based on a bit of truth.

"People talked about what you did to those kids. Such stories do not pop out of thin air. You must have done something wrong."

The man rests his head against the steel and states, "Do you ever stop your game and think? The people talking are spreading false information to get back at me. If any kid was hurt by anyone, then you need to search those talking for the person responsible."

Nicholas is surprised at the suggestion. However, the logic is not spectacular.

Nicholas replies, "If someone is doing this for vengeance, then you must have done something. I heard the stories while construction workers chatted with one another. Who did you piss off and how?"

The man looks up to him and states, "Agree to let me go and I will tell you anything you want to know about my life."

Nicholas laughs and replies, "You just killed my brief moment of thinking you may be innocent. Rather than give answers, you make demands. Hate to remind you, but you have no authority to demand anything. Now, tell me what you are guilty of committing."

The man slams the steel bars and yells, "I did not do a damn thing to any child!"

Nicholas watches him as he walks to the cot and drops down on it. The man picks up a bottle of water and holds it on his lap.

"If your statement is accurate, then why the rumor of sexual assault? Is there not another way to get revenge?"

The man begins unscrewing the cap on the bottle and replies, "Because apparently the punk bitch is not man enough to handle it any other way. And if the story sounds accurate, then they are probably hurting kids because I cannot even imagine creating a believable story like that."

"Ok, however, you would have had to do something terribly wrong for someone to look for revenge in such a way. What did you do?"

"I did not do shit!" yells the man as he throws the uncapped bottle of water towards Nicholas.

The bottle hits the steel bars as water flies through the air. Nicholas attempts to move to avoid the water, but still receives a few drops on his clothes. He knows the conversation tonight is getting no where.

"If you are not guilty of anything, how do you expect this to end? Am I to let you go?" Nicholas sarcastically asks.

"Just get it all over with and kill me. You know my death is your desire no matter what I tell you. You hide behind this freeing the world of sickos image. However, we both know you kill simply because you want to kill. You want death. So give it to me!"

"You are wrong." replies Nicholas.

He turns and walks away from the stool. Once he reaches the steps, he turns off the light and begins ascending. He needs to figure out how to reach this guy a bit better. His usual methods are not working.

The reason for all of this is to end the sick games. If these people would think about what it will cause them, then they would have to see the logic in not doing it. Why is it so hard to understand? Do these people not care about self preservation?

Nicholas shuts the door after exiting the stair well. He believes he shall up the challenge against this guy a bit starting tomorrow. Without food and water for a bit, he will more than likely begin talking. If he needs coercing after that, then he may need to rely on more traditional methods. He was never one to torture, but he may not have a choice. Definitely, a learning lesson for another day. For now, he will simply return home and go to bed.

Chapter 55

ANGELA LAUGHS AS PETER makes a mocking face towards Nicholas while preparing their evening meal. She takes a sip of her wine as Nicholas opens his beer and states, "Now, Peter, I believe such faces are an insult to your employer."

Peter rolls his eyes and states, "And tempting justification to the person making your meal is absolute stupidity. I can do a lot more to food than simply make it taste bad."

Nicholas chokes on his beer with laughter. Angela loves moments like this. The comedy of the friendship is so relaxing.

The door bell rings as Peter dices carrots. Angela wonders who has arrived. Nicholas did not tell her anyone was joining them.

"Nicholas, the meal will prepare faster if you continue dicing the carrots while I answer the door."

As Peter walks away, Nicholas shakes his head. Yet, he walks over to the carrots and begins dicing. Angela did not realize he even knew what dicing meant until now. She is going to have to learn a bit more about Nicholas's knowledge of a kitchen.

Angela hears a muffled conversation after Peter opens the door. Followed by a shout of "Where is he?" She looks to Nicholas as she wonders what is happening. He is no longer dicing the carrots. As he grips the knife, he stares towards the kitchen entryway as a nightmare is about to arrive. She is beginning to get very scared.

Two men rush in shining badges as they state, "FBI, Nicholas Payne we are here to question you. Please put the knife down and come with us."

Rather than replying or doing as they say, Nicholas moves the knife to his throat. Angela cannot believe what she is seeing. With the knife at his jugular, she worries he may cause major damage.

"Nicholas, do what they ask!" yells Angela.

He continues to look at the officers as he steps back from the counter. Angela turns to look at the officers in attempt to get assistance. The agents looks calm as one states, "Do not go this route, Mr. Payne. We simply need to talk with you."

"I doubt it will end there." states Nicholas as a drop of blood runs down his neck.

"That may be so. However, you need to think about what you are doing right now. Your beautiful girlfriend is sitting in front of you. She is worried about you and wants you to comply. Give her a positive memory rather than a bad one."

Angela feels tears run down her cheeks as Nicholas looks towards her. She cannot think of anything to say as he looks at her with regret. She simply does not understand what is happening.

"I love you, Angela."

As she hopes he is dropping the knife, Nicholas shuves it deep into his throat and falls to the ground as gurgling sounds are heard. Angela screams as the agents rush to his body and yell, "Call an ambulance!"

The agents begin attempt to stop the bleeding as Angela clings to the counter and prays this is simply a nightmare. She wants to wake up. She needs to wake up. This cannot be happening.

As she sees a stream of blood roll past the counter, she knows Nicholas is probably going to die. More agents rush in to assist as one calls for an ambulance.

"This is not happening. It cannot be happening." yells Angela.

A FBI agent walks to her and states, "Miss Summers, it is best if you come with me. They will do their very best to keep him alive. You do not want to see this."

Angela nods as her body trembles uncontrollably. The agent helps her stand as they walk out of the kitchen. Once led to a settee, Angela sits and continues shaking. The agent takes a blanket from someone and wraps it around her as she simply stares at the floor.

"She is in shock. Agents are working on keeping him alive. He shoved a knife through his neck." whispers the FBI agent.

As someone sits next to her, Angela does not bother to look. She wants the nightmare to end.

"Angela, I need you to stay with me. This is not how anyone wants this to go."

Hearing a familiar sound, Angela looks to the person sitting next to her and sees Javier.

"What is happening?" asks Angela.

"Nicholas has a lot of anger held inside from parents partaking in child pornography. We found a video of it at a murder victim's home. We also found a survellience video of him taking off with another victim, which allowed us the search warrant. Thankfully, the victim is still alive and in fairly good condition. Nicholas was keeping him in the basement of the house his office is located. Angela, Nicholas is our serial killer."

"No!" shouts Angela as she crumbles in grief.

Javier pulls her close to console her agony. She clings to him as tears stream down.

Javier rubs her head as he holds her close and states, "Angela, it is okay. Nicholas simply has issues from an unfair life. He is not the one to blame for all of it. He simply made bad choices in solving tragedy he endured."

Javier wishes he could flip a switch and ease her pain. However, it will not happen. He hates himself for not seeing all of this sooner. He cannot blame Nicholas for killing the people he did. Javier wishes daily people such as them would simply die so the pain of others would end. Unfortunately, pain simply changes form and causes more tragedy. He simply hopes the pain will not cause Angela to slip away as well.

Epilogue

FRED SITS DOWN AT HIS desk and awaits his first meeting. Life and business changed a lot after the passing of Nicholas Payne. He thought he hit a jackpot when Nicholas stepped into his office the first time. Most of his job began to consist of setting up trust funds to fund various organizations Nicholas set up. He wanted all to be secure if something happened to him. Hell, he even set up arrangements for the mansion and domestic violence victims cherish the opportunity to escape. Oddly, his victims and their families were handled through the one account Nicholas kept in his name. Thankfully, there was plenty to change the lives of all of them. He may have been a serial killer, but he had a heart of gold. Fred simply wishes he had opened up to someone about his pain.

"Your first appointment has arrived."

Fred looks to his intercom and replies, "Send her in."

Fred rises from his seat and walks towards the door as it opens. Angela Summers walks in with a look of hesitation. He imagines she is still attempting to piece together her life with Nicholas. He knows she will never find the answers she desires. No one will find the answer of what they could have done to keep Nicholas with him. He held all the power of the relationships.

"Welcome, Angela. Please take a seat." states Fred.

As Angela sits, Fred returns to his chair and thinks on what to say to make this conversation simple.

"I am sure you want to know why I asked you to my office. I simply need to speak with you on a matter Nicholas set up to assist you."

Angela shakes her head and states, "I do not need any money from his estate. I simply work towards moving on with life."

"No, Angela, it is nothing like that. You told Nicholas about your brother and he desired to help you find him. After getting so far with people Nicholas knew, I hired a private detective to track your brother down."

Angela feels as if she is on a game show and is given the choice to choose the right door to win. Why does this all have to have a positive ending? She met a man she was falling in love with only to lose him to himself. And then, after his death, all he cared about was left with blessings from his estate.

"Is my brother still alive?"

Fred smiles and replies, "Let me tell you a bit about where his life took him. As you know, he lived life here on the street. He became attached to a girl with an addiction problem. Your brother convinced her to move off with him and kick the addiction, which they did. However, the addiction did not go away. The girl overdosed and died."

Angela shakes her head as she looks to the ground. She asks, "Did he become an addict?"

"No, your brother never touched any of the drugs. After her death, he simply stayed with his job and lived life. He now is married with three kids. They do not live extravagant lives, but do not struggle too much either."

Fred slides a folder towards her and states, "Look in here. You will see pictures of him with the kids playing at a park. His wife was at work. So, the detective was unable to gather a picture of her."

Angela looks through the folder. She sees a picture of her brother laughing as the kids appear to dance around with snowcones. Two boys and a girl make his new title of dad. She wants to know them.

"Why did he never contact me?" asks Angela.

"I cannot answer that for you. However, you will notice the back of last picture notes his address and phone number. You have the chance to reach out to him."

Angela looks at the back of the picture and smiles. She imagines Skip simply does not want to subject his children to his father.

With a smile, Angela asks, "Is there anything else to discuss?"

"No, I simply wanted to give you the information."

Angela rises and shakes Fred's hand.

"Thank you. I shall cherish it."

After a smile and nod, Angela walks out of his office. She feels as if she is free from the questions that constantly plagued her through the years. She knows she still needs answers, but now they seem possible to obtain.

"How did it go?"

Angela looks to Javier and states, "Very well. I am an aunt. I simply need to meet them and make it official."

Javier chuckles as he stands and wraps his arm around her waist. As they begin walking out of the office, Angela wonders how she can thank Nicholas for this wonderful blessing. He has done so much for so many. Yet, no one could ease his pain.

He deserves something for all of it. And she will not let his efforts die. She will talk with her brother to find answers and discuss life. She has such a story to tell she doubts her brother will become bored. And, unlike their youth, he will not run to their parents to nark her out. After all that has happened, the world may begin to look normal again real soon.

Page

Don't miss out!

Visit the website below and you can sign up to receive emails whenever R. Gayle Hawkins publishes a new book. There's no charge and no obligation.

https://books2read.com/r/B-A-MAYC-INJV

BOOKS 2 READ

Connecting independent readers to independent writers.

Also by R. Gayle Hawkins

With Loyalty Came Love
The Strive for Life and Love
Treasure in the Past
Feline Moments
Amongst Death

Watch for more at rgaylehawkins.jimdo.com.

About the Author

R. Gayle Hawkins began her writing career in 2014 after disablement from Multiple Sclerosis. As a child, she often thought of writing, but life kept her from it.

She lives in Ohio.

Read more at rgaylehawkins.jimdo.com.

9 781393 471554